LONG WAY HOME

....

Meredith Richards

Contents

A ndrew Dwight "Dewy" Montgomery is headed back to Texas. A survivor among few, the last battle has been fought, and he is headed home. But, will he have a home to return to? His father disowned him when he left and his fiancee, Ellisa, broke their engagement. Three years later, this boy-turned-man arrives back in his hometown. What will he find when he gets there, and who will be left to welcome this hero home?

The Fading Drums of War

C olumbus, Georgia
1865

War. It was brutal. Blood, bones, guts, and screams that pierced the air, drowning out any human thought from his mind. Dewy fought to maintain his composure. Clem, his best friend, had been wounded and carried off, only to die in the hack job of a surgery they were trying to perform. The attempt to save his life had taken it.

His leg was bruised from a shallow gunshot wound, and Dewy had managed to pull the bullet from the flesh of his left thigh, thankful that it hadn't gone deep enough to need surgery. The doctors were merely cutting limbs off with a saw at this point, and too many men were dying from infection, fevers, and loss of blood. He said a thankful prayer to the Almighty for preserving him.

With little else to do, he offered to assist in burying the dead. As a low ranking soldier, he would've been told to do it anyway. Not a task he wanted, but someone had to, and he was alive do so. Even as he went about the self-appointed task, Dewy wondered about the folks back home. How long would it be before the families of these many men learned of their demise? The grieving mothers, the mourning widows: Their lives were changed forever because of this bloody battle that ended all battles.

What did a soldier with a musket and rank on his shirt do at the end of a war? Did he just pick up and go home? Men called out from every direction, sending orders, making plans. Dewy stood over the grave of a man, a boy really, who was too young to die in battle. He'd never know the love of a woman, the cry of his firstborn, or the labor of providing for a family. Dewy's silent prayer went up for the boy, his family, and himself.

"YOU THERE!" An unknown Sergeant called out. "HURRY UP! THERE'S MORE TO BURY." Dewy snapped to attention and moved on to the next one, thinking the same thoughts, praying the same prayers, and pouring the dirt from the shovel over corpse after corpse as tears flowed down his face. He did this until sunset without stopping except to drink every now and again.

Little Comfort

Comfort, Texas

One Month Later

The news of the war's end travelled slowly, but finally, the list had made its way to the small town of Comfort, Texas. Ellisa Townsend rushed to the town's square to see the names of those dead and missing in action. She prayed she wouldn't find his. She stood in line with the other onlookers: People who cared about one another, went to church together, helped bring in each other's crops, and enjoyed the simple life.

A gut-wrenching cry went out, followed by another, as citizens of the little town found, one by one, the names of their sons, husbands, brothers, and friends on the list.

Ellisa noticed that Douglas and Mary Jenkins were next to look. Their son was in the same company as Dewy. Mary's loud scream, followed by sobs, told Ellisa all she needed to know: Clem Jenkins,

Dewy's best friend, was dead. Ellisa broke from the line to comfort Mary and Douglas, and their daughter, Emma.

Emma, surprisingly, wasn't crying. She looked instead like she'd seen someone trampled by a horse. She didn't move or speak until their eyes met. "He's not on the list, Ellisa. He's not on it. Dewy's name... it's not there. Maybe he's still..." Then she was engulfed in her friend's arms as the sobs began to rip through her like a sharp stick through a pair of thin pants.

After a few long moments of attempting to comfort her friend, Emma waved and walked back to the wagon with her parents to go grieve in privacy. Ellisa's heart pounded in her chest. She believed Emma. She really did, but she had to investigate for herself; she had to be sure his name wasn't there.

Her memories took her to the day he left. He sure looked handsome in his uniform as he prepared to leave. He'd been trained, and then returned home to say goodbye to his parents, his siblings, and to her. In her resentment, Ellisa had decided she couldn't be engaged to a man who probably would not return alive. Of course, there were not many other men to think about, as most had volunteered. His face had twisted at her words. Hurt poured from every part of him, but he'd kissed her goodbye.

"I promise you I'll come back and I'll marry you when I do." He whispered as he lowered his face to hers one final time.

"I can't promise that I'll wait for you. In case you haven't heard, men are dying and by the thousands. What am I to do if I wait for you and you return in a pine box? Marry a corpse? It's not fair to ask that of me, Dewy. It just isn't."

Dewy touched her cheek softly with the back of his knuckle, moved a wayward curl away from her face, and smiled his devilishly handsome smile. His eyes were so blue, she could look at the sky and it would pale in comparison. He was fair-haired and taller than most of the other boys in the town. She'd fallen almost instantly in love with him. Now he was leaving her for a cause; going off to fight a war that should not be happening, according to his Paw.

"I love you, Ellisa. I will return." He said with one final touch, squeezing her hand in his just before he ran off to join the other men heading out by train.

Returning her thoughts to the present, she realized she had made her way to the front and was able to read for herself the names on the list. Alphabetically, they were listed. She began to skim the names, stifling back many a tear, of men she knew: Anderson, Carmichael, Donovan, Franc, Holloman, Ingalls, and Jenkins. She paused when she saw Clem's name. A wayward tear escaped before she could catch it. Ellisa continued reading: Klein, Lancaster. Oh no! Emma knew the name Klein meant somthing to Dewy. His sister, Mary, was married to a boy named Klein. She prayed it wasn't Mary's husband. All of the deceased were boys she'd gone to school with, their brothers, their fathers; all dead. How would tiny Comfort, Texas, ever rebound from a loss as great as this? She was finally to the "M's." She read them aloud, softly.

"Matthias, Miller, Monroe, Murphy. No Montgomery." She took in a shuddered breath."No Montgomery. He's not on the list." Her hopes soared even as she wiped her tears away. She didn't know if she was willing to marry him, but at least he was alive as far as anyone knew.

Turning to go, Ellisa spotted Gaius Montgomery in the line. She ran up to him, smiling. "He's not on the list, Mr. Montgomery. We still have hope." She said, hugging Miss Tilly, Dewy's mom, as she said it. Tilly nodded silently, covering her mouth with her hands as a sob caught in her throat. She waved goodbye to Ellisa before turning to her husband.

~~~~~

Gaius Montgomery didn't show any emotion. He was still, three years later, angry that his boy went against his wishes. Maybe that was a long time to hold onto a grudge, but he wasn't about to compromise his beliefs. Others in this town had also gone, and where had it landed them? In the grave. He was relieved to hear that his son was alive, but Andrew would not be allowed back in his house again. He'd deliberately disobeyed and gone off to fight. His mother cried nightly in her concern for him, and prayed fervently for his safe return.

"Tilly, shall we go?" Gaius asked. He'd only come to check the list on her urging, and now that they knew his name wasn't there, they were free to proceed with their day to day tasks.

Matilda, Tilly to everyone who knew her personally, shrugged and wiped a silent tear from her cheek. At least, for now, she could rest and know her boy was safe. It wasn't so easy for his friend's family, or many others in this town, but he may come home yet. Her hopes of reconciliation between Dewy and her husband brought fresh tears to her eyes. The man she'd married, and loved, was now a hard-hearted person. He only showed tenderness towards her in their private time together. She hadn't seen him smile ten times since Andrew marched off.

Tilly made up in her mind that she would pray her son home that day and she had not wavered even once from her goal. Now, she hoped, he was on his way back to her. Gaius would come around, she was sure of it. Maybe she would have to pray for him, more than she already did, to welcome their only son back into his arms and their home. Otherwise, he may die a hurt, old man with no one to love because he drove them all away.

~~~~~

Dewy awoke in a puddle of his own sweat. He'd been dreaming; dreaming about home, about Ellisa, about his father and mother, and the long road from Austin to Comfort. He knew in his mind the journey could take more than a week of walking, but, all the same, his heart wanted to fly over the countryside directly to his backyard.

His dreams most nights were of the bodies, the blood, the screams, and the horrors of war. But last night had been different, and he thanked the Good Lord for that blessing. Too many nights, the battle waged on in his subconscious mind. Ellisa's beautiful face, dark hair and light green eyes floated before his mind's eye. He missed her so. He'd written a letter to her every month while he was gone, but he understood her silence, and remitted it to the fact that she was no longer his girl. Letters during war were not often received, and only then if they were able to locate a soldier.

The South had not fared well. In fact, they had lost terribly. He supported the North, because, unlike most towns in Texas, Comfort had supported the Union. It had been settled by abolitionists in the late 1850's and was still growing. His father had not supported the war from either side. This was the whole reason for their estrangement. His days of youth long past, Dewy prayed they could reconcile, but doubted as well.

"Faith has no room for doubt." His mother used to tell him when he was a boy. He could hear her voice so clearly, he would've sworn she was sitting behind him. He missed his mother so. He knew his life was held up solely by her prayers. Returning to her would be bittersweet if his father refused to recognize his existence. He found a way to pen a letter, informing them that he was indeed still alive and returning to Comfort post-haste.

The idea that he was returning gave him a reason to smile. He would win his father's heart again. They had been so close before. He was sure that would return once his father saw him safe and sound at home.

Released just yesterday, he was anxious to get back, but with the railroads incapacitated in so many areas, the journey would be much longer than the several days it took by train. He hoped for coaches, but was resigned to walking for most of his journey. Maybe he'd be home by Christmas, Lord willing. Dewy sighed as he rolled his sleeping gear and what little food he had and started walking West, with the sun at his back, towards home. A silent prayer went to heaven that he would be welcomed with open arms when he did finally arrive.

Middle of Nowhere

Dewy had been walking for days, stopping to sleep. If he caught a rabbit or a squirrel, he ate. Otherwise, he only drank. He was glad for the hunting skills he had developed as a boy. At least he wouldn't starve completely.

Somewhere along the way, he had come across an abandoned homestead. There he'd found some canned provisions, clothing, and other necessary items he needed to aid his journey some. Now most of that had been spent, but at least he'd changed from his uniform. People didn't take kindly to Yankee soldiers; especially Southern sympathizers who'd fought for the North. He'd likely end up shot if someone found him walking in a U.S. uniform instead of a haphazard looking Southern one.

He had a hunting knife, the one his Paw had given him on his twelfth birthday, that he kept in his boot for emergencies, but he'd shucked his rifle a while back. That was an identifier. He'd found a pistol in another place, but no ammunition to speak of. Those were hard to come by, much less the bullets to use them, but he'd kept it anyway.

The truth of the whole matter was this: He had no idea where he was, but he was sure it was the way home.

~~~~~

As night began to fall, and the sky darkened, Dewy happened upon a small abode with a barn in the back. The farm lands had been burned. Shameful. He decided to say hello as he walked past.

Waving his arm, he greeted the older lady and gentleman seated on their porch. They were smiling, laughing, and talking like the worst possible thing hadn't just happened around them.

"Good e'en." The man said, waving back. "You needin' a meal? The wife here's got a stew on and some fresh bread." Dewy loved the country and the folks in it. They were just friendlier here.

"I'd be much obliged. Say, any idea where I am? I've been walking for two weeks. Came from Georgia; headin' home to Texas."

"A soldier?" The woman asked, putting her hands on her face in shock. "Why, we lost our son and grandson while they were fighting at Antietam. You come on in and sit a spell."

The man piped in. "Yes, little old Luverne (he said it like Loo-Vun instead of Luh-vern), Alabama has lost many of her native sons. You're more than welcome to eat at table with us and stay over. Restore for a spell before headin' on; that's what you need to do."

"I much appreciate the offer. These feet sure are tired." Dewy exclaimed as he rested his laurels on their porch step.

The lady disappeared into the house briefly, coming out with bread and a cup in her hands. "Fresh lemonade? Here's a little something to eat. That should tide you over until dinner."

"I surely do appreciate your hospitality. Name's Andrew. Andrew Montgomery; but everyone who knows me calls me Dewy." He stuck his hand out to shake the man's hand, and then kissed the back of the woman's wrinkled hand, as well.

"Otis and Tiva Brown. Nice to make your acquaintance, Mr. Montgomery. Please, do come in and rest a bit."

Dewy smiled, wiped his brow with this shirt sleeve, before resting his pack on their front porch and following them in to the modest cabin. It was really a one-room house, with a loft built over the main area for sleeping. They were modest accommodations, but Dewy learned at a young age that a beggar couldn't afford to be picky. He was happy he could receive a home-cooked meal.

"Here's some water to wash up with. We have a small cot in the cellar. Otis will get if for you after we finish eating." Tiva explained.

"If you don't mind, I can get it, Ma'am. I don't want him going out of his way for a passerby." Dewy really didn't want the elderly man moving anything. He looked like he was more frail than a newborn.

"Otis doesn't mind a'tall. He's proud to help one of our Southern boys." Tiva waved him off. Dewy didn't bother to correct her. She'd probably shoo him out with a broom and that shotgun over the hearth if she knew he fought with the Yankees. No, he'd just as soon keep quiet and appreciate their hospitality, asking forgiveness to God for the omission of truth.

~~~~~

In the morning, Dewy politely folded up their cot, placing it back from where Otis had brought it. He washed his face, accepted Tiva's meager food offerings, and picked up his bag. With his apologies for the early departure, and many thank you's, Dewy set off, once again walking away from the sun.

His letter would be taken to the nearest town, but whether or not it ever reached his Ma, he couldn't say. The system was past broken. It was destroyed: A tactic the Yankees had deployed to slow the South down.

Many were still hostile, and most every family on both sides was grieving a loss. Dewy tried not to think about those who wouldn't be returning with him. In fact, he wondered if he was the only hometown son headed home on his own two feet. He thought about Clem Jenkins, his parents, and Ellisa. She was always in the forefront of his mind. His father was next, and Dewy said a prayer that the man would soften his heart and be willing to allow Dewy back.

That thought was on an endless loop in his mind. He kept thinking on it. He couldn't let it go no matter how hard he tried until the idea switched places with the image of Ellisa. He'd think of her lovely face, the flavor of her kiss, the feelings in his heart when he held her close, until he wanted to scream. She was his heart and soul. He prayed she would accept him again.

One phrase made its way into the forefront of his brain: Going to war had ruined his life. Shaking his head, he kept walking. No, it hadn't. Going to war had been the only choice. Every capable man was needed. His father had decided not to go to war, and Dewy was glad for it for one simple reason: If they'd both gone and died, she'd be left alone. His father's body wouldn't have been able to handle battle anyway. He'd been injured as a teen in a serious horse and buggy incident. He wasn't supposed to be able to have children, but Ma married him anyway. Dewy was the youngest son of four. The doctors had thankfully been very wrong. Dewy had an older brother, an older sister, and a twin sister. Now, his sisters, Emma, his twin, and Mary, were married with and children. Emma had married William Logan and Mary was married to Joseph Klein. His brother Philip was still in Comfort, but never really had many dealings with his parents. Still, they considered him the "good" son who agreed with Paw on the war. Dewy wondered if maybe Philip was near and more present to them now that Dewy had chosen the "wrong path."

He prayed for his two sisters and Philip, as well as his Ma and Paw. He prayed for Emma and Mary's husbands who had gone off to war. He'd hate to see them widowed so young. Joseph and William were boys from Comfort, but had enlisted before Dewy, so they had been in different Regiments.

The next town wasn't more than half a day's journey, and by noon, Andrew was hot as he approached it. He stopped under a shady oak and took a little of the food Miss Tiva had given him from his satchel. Thanking God for the provisions, he ate and rested a while before continuing on. He'd be in Mississippi in another day or two.

A smile formed on his unshaven face. He was that much closer to home. Maybe he could find a way to travel some on what trains were running, or find a coach to take him part of the way. Until then, he'd keep walking.

The Letter

Tilly Montgomery had finally found time to visit in town. She'd just left the home of Doug and Mary Jenkins when none other than Ellisa Townsend came running towards her, waving a paper in her hand like she had some big news to share.

"Mrs. Montgomery, I'm so glad I caught you." Ellisa began breathlessly. As she recovered, she continued. "This came for you. Mr. Alberty said to get it to you fast. It's from Dewy." Hubert Alberty was the general store owner. Mail was delivered to his shop if for some reason the delivery could not be made to the recipient's home. Tilly wondered why it had not been taken to their home.

"Really?" Tilly smiled. "I've been waiting to hear from him."

Ellisa blushed and sighed. "I have a letter, too. Though, I'm not sure what to make of it. He talked of Clem and some of the other men who died, but then he said he looked forward to our wedding, like we were still getting married. Tilly, what do I make of it?"

"He misses you is all. I'm sure that's it, dear. I am going to read this bit of news in front of my hearth, I believe. I will pass any information along that needs to be shared. I'm happy you've received a letter, too, dear. Is there hope for the two of you when he makes it back?" Tilly asked, distracted by the passersby and the content of her letter.

"I think I will have to wait and see. I won't know until he gets here." Ellisa responded half-heartedly. "I'm sure no matter what happens, we'll still be friends. I hope that's enough."

"We have to remember to forgive like the Lord does us. No matter how much he's hurt us, we have to love him for the sake of all things Holy." Tilly smiled, giving the young woman a surprising hug. She wasn't such a young woman any more, at the age of twenty-one. Most women were married by eighteen at the latest. Tilly still thought of Ellisa as her daughter-in-law even though the girl had chosen not to marry when Dewy left for war. The poor dear, Tilly thought. She'd be an old spinster because of her love for him.

Bidding a goodbye wave, Tilly headed for home.

Ellisa didn't respond to Tilly's admonition about loving Dewy. She'd loved him since the day they met, when she was twelve. Dewy would always be the only boy with whom she wanted to dance, kiss, love until death. His face came to the forefront of her mind, and she headed for her parents' home, hoping no one saw the tears streaming down her face.

~~~~~

Tilly walked up the lane, heading home. Philip, her oldest son, greeted her from the porch before she'd ever reached it.

"Why, hello, son. What brings you today?" She smiled, handing her small bag of goods to him. She'd managed to do a little shopping and had some cloth she was going to embroider for a new dining table covering.

"I needed to check on a few things. Paw asked me to come by for today, but he doesn't seem to be about. Would you know where he is?" Philip's query fell on half-deaf ears as Tilly thought about the letter she had to read and about how Gaius would react to it. "Maw?"

"Oh, he may be out in the stables, or checking on something further out on the property. Would you like to come in for lemonade and cookies while you wait? I miss having you boys around." She responded wistfully.

"I'd love to come in. You'd have us both if Dewy had listened to Paw." Philip's words were laced with disdain for his brother's actions. "I mean, I understand, but ..."

"Now, Philip, we must remember that the Lord has forgiven him already, and we have to follow his example. I was just saying the same thing to Miss Townsend when she handed me Dewy's letter." Instantly, Tilly wished she could recant that last statement. She didn't want anyone else to know about it until she'd had time to read it through. She wanted to prepare Gaius for the news, and not just thrust the letter in his face after dinner. Unfortunately, Philip had very keen ears.

"You received a letter from our wayward boy? Pray-tell, how is he?" Philip looked genuinely concerned, a complete turnaround from a moment before.

"I don't know. I wanted to read it when I settled for the day. Don't tell your father about this. I will break the news to him when we're alone for the evening. Understand, son?"

Philip kissed his mother's cheek before carrying the tray of cookies and lemonade to the table. "Yes Ma'am. My lips are sealed. But, I am concerned he'll want to come back and behave like he never left, and that may make things difficult for you and Paw."

"When my son comes home, I'll welcome him with open arms, and you'd do well to emulate me. Our Lord told a story about this very thing. We're to forgive and love. The Lord instructed us to do that much, and I won't fail my Lord or my son."

Philip said not another word. He wasn't so sure about forgiving and forgetting where Dewy was concerned, but he wouldn't get into a scuffle of words with his mother over it. She would only, could only see one outcome, and that was Dewy back in her home, safe, smiling, and alive.

~~~~~

Ellisa sat at the table in front of her mother's cook stove, tears streaming from her eyes. Dewy's letter had been so long, especially for Dewy, and so heartfelt. She couldn't believe the things he'd said. Dewy had never been a man of many words, unless something was important to him, but in this letter, he'd placed everything on the line. He confessed his unending love, spoken of the horrors of war, and Clem's death, his reconciliation with the Almighty, and his hope of a future with Ellisa. Then he talked about reuniting with his family. He hoped she would be an ambassador of sorts between him and them. This was where Ellisa wasn't sure she could intervene. Gaius wasn't known for his kindness or being easily persuaded. Ellisa had not told Tilly Montgomery all of the contents. She didn't want to disclose the private aspects of Dewy's heart, and figured Tilly would probably be as upset as she was now.

Ellisa thought to their courtship and engagement. She'd prayed throughout his time at war that no matter how things had ended, he would survive. Now that she knew he had, she wondered if they could salvage the comfortable and easy relationship they used to have. She'd never stopped loving Dewy, if she was being honest with herself, and according to his letter, he still felt the same way as the day he'd left. She had a decision to make, but didn't want to think about it until she saw him face-to-face.

~~~~~

Gaius Montgomery eyed his wife suspiciously. She'd been too quiet during dinner, and even during devotion time. Something was wrong, but what he wasn't sure. He'd earned a reputation for being a hard man, and in his mind he had every right to feel and think the way he did. The Good Lord didn't make man to war with one another. However, here, in their bedroom, Gaius Montgomery was not that hard man. He loved his wife with a passion that he poured into his whole life. Maybe that's why people thought he was hard. Things were a certain way. His love for Matilda Louise Atwater Montgomery made him do things he otherwise wouldn't even consider. The woman knew exactly how to sway him, and he'd let her keep on as long as they both lived.

Yes, life with Tilly was peaceful. Except for tonight. She was not at peace. In fact, he knew without doubt that it had something to do with that wayward boy. He'd get to the bottom of the barrel, so to speak, and he'd do it tonight.

Quietly, he crossed the room to help her with her buttons. "When are you going to tell me what's bothering you, Tilly?" He asked, kissing her shoulder as he unbuttoned her dress.

Tilly didn't respond, not even to his kisses. She said nothing, but slipped into her dressing gown before going to turn down the bed. Gaius grabbed her hand as she walked by, stopping her still and tilting her head until their eyes met. He smoothed back a wayward strand of hair with his thumb. Tilly was shut down inside. He silently vowed to help her lift her burden. "Til... you gonna tell me why you're so contemplative tonight?" His eyes bore into hers and they shone with concern.

"I will as soon as we're a-bed." She responded before walking to her dresser to place her one piece of jewelry, other than her simple wedding band, in the drawer. It was a string of pearls her boys and husband had collectively bought her for her fortieth birthday. She smiled when she touched it, and wore it every time she went into town for anything.

Gaius, not one to be turned away where the marital bed was concerned, wandered up behind her, wrapped one arm around her waist and pulled her to him. "I know something's bothering you, and until I know what it is, I won't let you be. Besides, I had a mind to love on you for quite some time tonight." He smiled as he once again kissed her neck, sending a shiver up her spine. Gaius turned his wife around and looked down into her eyes. "Is it news of Andrew?" He never called his child by his nickname. It was always the proper name. The only person by whom he called a shortened name of any type was his wife. It spoke of intimacy, and he didn't want to be intimate with anyone as much as he was with her.

At his question, Tilly turned her face into his shoulder and began to sob; softly at first, but then her tears intensified until her whole body was shaking.

"It is Andrew. Is he alive? Is Dewy alive, Tilly?" For the first time in longer than he cared to admit, his tough exterior cracked. The very idea that Andrew had died weakened his hardened heart.

"Yes, he is." Tilly whispered softly.

"Oh, thank the Lord." At her husband's exclamation, Tilly leaned her head back from his shoulder and peered unbelieving into his face. Had he really just thanked God out loud for their son's safety?

"At least, as of when this letter was written, he was. You need to read it, Gaius. You need to read it tonight before you slumber. Then, you need to pray. My boy... he's ... coming ... home." She surrendered to her tears again, and sturdy, hard, Gaius Montgomery pulled her to his shoulder ... just in time for an unnoticed tear to slide down his own cheek unchecked.

The Farm

Six weeks had passed since Dewy left Luverne, Alabama. He'd come across many kind folks on his journey. He'd been through Hattiesburg, and remembered thinking it a hostile town, for certain. Now, another week had passed and he was sure he was halfway through Mississippi. As he traveled on, he passed a sign:

Welcome to Jackson, Mississippi.

"Jackson? Oh boy!" Dewy thought to himself: "I'm deep in Rebel country now." He passed through the town about the supper hour, but moved on, hoping to make it to the outbound road before night-fall.

His goal achieved, Dewy pressed for the homestead he viewed in the distance. Not more than another hour's walk and he'd make it there. Maybe they'd allow him to sleep in the barn, out of the weather that was brewing on the horizon.

"Hello!" He waved and called to the man on the porch.

"Howdy, stranger. Looks like it may rain. Need a place for the night?" The man said, sticking his hand out as Dewy approached.

"Come on in." He walked with a cane, as he was missing a leg, and hobbled slowly towards the house. "The Mrs. is working on supper. I hope you like chicken. It's about all we have now. Most of my cows died in the drought last summer and the Union decided they needed 'em more than me, so they took much of what was left. Why on earth would a troop of soldiers need a herd of cattle? Anyway, we have a few left, but mostly for milk. We're raising chickens and hogs, and hopefully we'll be able to put up enough for the coming winter. Where you coming from?"

Dewy smiled, glad to have a person to converse with instead of his own thoughts for company. "I left Georgia two months ago. I'm heading home to Texas now. It's a bit of a trip, I'll say."

Mr. Monroe nodded. "Indeed it is. A horse would do you some good."

"Yes, sir, it would, but I'm grateful to the Good Lord for my life and legs. I'll get there, by and by."

"What's your name, soldier?"

"Andrew Montgomery. It's a pleasure to meet you." He held a hand out to shake.

"Pleasures all mine, Montgomery. The name's Lawrence Monroe." He took Dewy's pack and placed it in a small room off the main family room. "Guest room's in there, and you're more than welcome to stay the night. It'll do my wife some good to have a strapping young man in the home again. Our youngest was your age. I'm guessing you're about twenty?"

"Yes, sir." Dewy chuckled at the odd turn in conversation. The man seemed eager to have a man's company.

"Our boys, all five of 'em, went to war. None of 'em survived. Our oldest three were married with children, so we're blessed to have our grandchildren. It still hurts my wife to think that none of her boys are coming home, though. How was it? The war, I mean?"

"I'd rather not say, sir. It was dreadful. I saw too many dead, including my best friend. The Almighty saw fit to preserve me, so I dwell on that; no sense remembering the bad stuff." He surmised.

"Very true. Say, tomorrow's Sunday. Would you care to attend church with us?"

"I haven't stepped foot in a church in months. I greatly appreciate the offer. That way, when I get to my Maw, she won't be hounding me about not going for so long." Dewy chuckled, and then Mr. Monroe let out a guffaw that shook his whole being, making Dewy laugh harder.

"I imagine you are right, there, son. We're glad to have you. Let me see if she's ready for dinner. Catherine? We've company. Do you have enough for one more?" He said in a slightly raised voice.

"Yes." A weak response came from another room. "There's plenty here." A petite, round woman came through the doorway.

"Catherine, have you been crying again?" Mr. Monroe asked in a sensitive and caring tone.

"Of course not, dear; just a bit sentimental. This was Everett's favorite meal, you know?"

"Catherine, I don't think there's a meal you can make that won't remind you of someone. Come meet our company before dinner. This is Mr. Andrew Montgomery. He's headed home from the war."

Catherine's eyes brimmed with unshed tears. "I am very glad to welcome you to our home. The wash basin and pitcher are in the small room off the kitchen. Feel free to wash up before dinner. My, you look the same age as Everett. He was twenty."

"Yes, Ma'am. I am turning two and twenty the day after Christmas."

"Say, do you need some clothes? He left behind quite a bit. I've already kept out what I want to, and the rest is just taking up space." She gushed over him, as if her son had returned from the war instead of a stranger.

"Thank you, Ma'am." Dewy bowed slightly, embarrassed at the attention, and excused himself to wash up.

~~~~~

The next morning, Dewy donned the clothing of their deceased son. He felt odd and even wondered if he'd met the young man during battle. There really wasn't a way to know. Dewy figured he'd find out on that day when he finally faced the Almighty for his own judgment.

Mrs. Monroe had eggs and biscuits ready for him when he joined them for breakfast. He hadn't had eggs for breakfast in so long, he had trouble remembering when.

"This is delicious, Mrs. Monroe." He said between hasty bites.

"Thank you, but please call me Catherine." She smiled a shy grin, and stood to pour more milk.

"I can't do that, Ma'am." He laughed, thanking her for the drink. "My Maw would tan my hide."

"Then, call me Miss Catherine. I'm no uppity woman to contend with. We're simple country folks who love Jesus and our neighbor, like the Good Book says." She exhorted as she sat to partake of her own plate. "A few more minutes and we'll be leaving for church. We're having a picnic on the church grounds afterwards. I hope you like picnics. I can say, the young women in the church will be falling over you. Maybe you should settle here and get married. We don't have many men anymore. It would do our town some good to have more young'uns around."

"Miss Catherine, the picnic sounds great. I won't be staying too long in Jackson, though. I have a girl whose heart I need to win back in my hometown. She's the only girl I see. Thank you, though." He chuckled again, amused at her suggestion to stay and marry locally.

Ellisa's dark hair and pale eyes floated before him again. He wondered if she'd changed much over the last few years. He was sure she had. She was only seventeen when he left for war. He'd missed her birthday just a few weeks back. He'd write to her tonight.

~~~~~

Catherine Monroe had been right about one thing: The girls were absolutely smitten by Dewy. They giggled, waved, stared, fanned, and a few brave ones introduced themselves. He'd probably met fifteen women over the course of the afternoon. Some seemed a little too eager, and others too shy. Some were beautiful, and some were plain, but all were cordial. If he knew any young men looking for brides, he would most certainly send them to Jackson.

He enjoyed the day and all of the festivities that came with it. The children played tag and held a three-legged race before calling it a day. The women had a baking contest, which Mrs. Monroe entered and won third place for her apple dumplings, and the men played horseshoes and had a sawing competition, which Dewy entered and won. The winner received a horse. Dewy looked up and praised the Lord for His provisions. At the end of the day, he rode his new mare, named Bess, back to the Monroe homestead.

"Andrew, I have a question for you." Lawrence asked as they put the horses in the barn and began brushing them down for the night.

"What would you like to know, Mr. Lawrence?" Dewy questioned with confusion and curiosity battling for the attention in his mind.

"Welp, I was wonderin' if you'd like to stay and help me with my hay and harvest before headin' on. My son-in-law is working on his own land, and you already know about the sad demise of our own children. I'm needin' a strong young man to help with some of the harder chores for a bit. Some of the other farmers will be along to help in another week or two, but there are some crops and fields that need immediate attention. Would you be innerested? There's pay, though not much, and of course we'll feed ya and all of that while you're here."

"Let me think and pray on it." Dewy said simply.

"Fair enough. I know you must be anxious to get back to your folks. Do they know you made it out alive?" His question was all too serious.

"I sent a letter to my Maw and Paw, and one to my girl, back when I was in Alabama. I'm writing home again tonight. I'll mention it if and when I decide to stay. I'm still so surprised at the horse! The Lord sure saw a need and provided!"

"He always does, son. He always does!" Lawrence repeated as they finished up in the stable and headed for the house.

~~~~~

After the Monroes had retired to their upstairs room for the evening, Dewy sat alone in their guest room, quill pen in hand. He thought, prayed, and thought some more. He imagined the conversation he'd have with his parents, if they were still speaking to him, and with Ellisa. No doubt his mother would want him home and soon. He had no idea which way Ellisa would go, but he hoped she'd want him to return swiftly. His father, in Dewy's mind's eye, would tell him a man had to make his own way, even if it meant delaying his home-coming to provide for himself; it was the right thing to do.

"You've got to have integrity, boy. If you don't have that, you have nothing." His father would say. "You have to earn your keep. Don't ever just take charity from someone without at least making a contribution in some way. Even if a person won't take the help offered outright, you find something that says you appreciate the kindness given. It will keep your good name. Trust me on this one, Andrew. I've seen many a stranger, helped many a man, and the ones I remember are the ones who help. I remember those who took advantage, too, and I'm not so keen on assisting them a second time unless it is a dire situation." His father's words were so real in his mind that Dewy could swear he was in the next room. He missed his Paw.

Ellisa would say: "Do what you need to, Dewy. I'll be here when you get back." In fact, she'd said that when he'd gone off on a round up a year before he left. She was always there with a beautiful smile on her face when he returned. He'd take her on a stroll after dinner, or sit in the parlor at either family's home and talk until someone told them it was getting late. He pined for those days of innocence.

Shaking his head to clear it, he started his first letter. He prayed that his Paw would forgive him, that his Maw would understand, and that his girl would welcome him back.

Discovered

Another letter reached Ellisa Townsend. Emma Jenkins hand delivered it that afternoon.

"Elle ... it's from Dewy." She used the familiar name that Dewy used to call her when they were teens.

"Oh, my! I don't know if I can handle any more right now. Every letter speaks of our future: A future I wasn't sure we would have when he left. And now he wants to resurrect our feelings and courtship. I'm not sure I can, Emma. I'm just not sure." She turned away to prepare the vegetables for the evening meal, and to subdue her emotions.

"Listen to me, Ellisa. This man loves you. He says so every time you receive a letter. At this point, unless I go elsewhere, I'll never marry. Joseph Carmichael was the closest thing I ever came to a courtship, and he's dead. You can't push away what's right in front of you. Promise me, Ellisa. Promise me you'll pray about him, think about him, entertain the idea of Dewy coming back to you; because that's exactly what he's doing: Coming back to you."

"You know, it seems everyone wants this but me. Not that I don't love him. I do!" She turned around, surprising Emma with her tears. Her lips and chin quivered with her feelings. "With my whole being, I love Dewy. But, he left anyway." She stopped momentarily, burying her face in her hands and sobbed. Before Emma could comfort her, she continued her diatribe. "My love wasn't strong enough to keep him back then. Who's to say it will be now? Even while vowing his undying devotion, he's delayed his homecoming to help some stranger in Mississippi. I have to wonder if he is as anxious to return as his letters suggest. Thank you for bringing the letter, and for being a dear friend." She returned to her task, saying nothing more.

Emma, unsure what to do or say, she left without another word to Ellisa. When the door shut, Ellisa stopped cutting the vegetables and sat at the small table in the summer kitchen and cried. She wept like a woman who'd learned of her love's demise instead of his well-being. A few minutes passed before she could control herself. That is when she opened the letter.

My Dearest Elle,

I have been in Mississippi a fortnight now. As you know already, my days are quite busy helping Mr. and Mrs. Monroe on the farm. He has only one leg, and all of his sons died in the War. I agreed to stay on, and they compensate me with pay, room and board, and some of the best cooking I've had in years. The couple is very good to me, treating me as if I am their own child. The whole town seems that way. They act as if I'm some sort of hero. I can't force myself to tell them I may responsible for the deaths of their sons, brothers, fathers, and husbands. I'd probably be stoned to death if they ever found out I wasn't a Confederate.

My nights are troubling. I have dreams so real, I feel like I'm still in battle. I wake up scared, defensive, and ready to do combat. Those are the bad ones. The good dreams? They're about you. I miss you so much at times that it hurts to think about what we had. I hope you can find it in your heart to forgive me. I dream of coming back to your open arms. Please say you'll think on it. I have never, for a moment, stopped loving you. You are my reason for coming home.

I shall be leaving in another week or two at most. I have a horse now. I won Bess in the sawing competition at the social gathering a few weeks ago. She will shorten my journey considerably. Look for me. It won't be long.

All my love now and always,

Andrew "Dewy" Montgomery

Ellisa laughed at the fact that he had to sign his full name instead of just "Dewy" when he signed off. She was glad for the laugh. Crying had her spent. Shaking her head, she stood to finish the meal she'd begun preparing.

~~~~~

Dewy awoke out of breath and sweating, again. He'd been dreaming. Too many nights in a row, the battles replayed in his mind; so lifelike, at times, he almost reached for a weapon to defend himself. He even hollered out some nights, waking Mr. and Mrs. Monroe. Lawrence would come and check to see if he was alright, and Dewy would always wave him off. Unless a man had been in a battle, he could not possibly understand the experience and the after-effects of it.

One morning, too early, Dewy was shoveling hay and cleaning stalls; his breath white in the pre-dawn cold. He stopped to wipe his brow and drink a sip of the coffee Mrs. Lawrence had on hand every morning, though it had cooled considerably. The smell of the hay, horses, and dew on the grass invigorated him. He was truly a farmer's child, and looked forward to having his own place someday.

"Got a minute, Son?" Lawrence asked, bringing a fresh steaming cup into the barn and offering it to Dewy.

"My time is yours, Lawrence. What's on your mind?" Dewy asked, bewildered at the impromptu conversation so early in the day. He nodded his silent thanks for the steaming cup that would chase the cool of the morning.

"I was wondering; I think I'd like to hear about your battles; where you fought and all of that." Lawrence sat on a bundle of hay across from the stall where Dewy worked.

Dewy's heart stopped for a brief moment; or so he thought upon hearing that question. "It's not something I care to talk about."

"I recognize some things and I want to help you."

"What do you know of it, Lawrence?" Dewy asked, moving back to the hay he was shoveling with renewed vigor. Indignation rose in his belly at the questions, and the idea that he needed help chafed his pride.

"I know more than you think." Lawrence responded.

That singular sentence forced Dewy to stick the pitch fork into the hay. Turning quickly, he narrowed his gaze onto the older man. Forgetting manners momentarily, he pinned the man visually to his prickly straw seat. After a deep breath, he regained his composure.

"I don't care to discuss my experiences at war. It was a horrible thing."

"It is that." Lawrence responded simply.

"What do you know of war?" Dewy asked more cynically than he'd meant. "My apologies; it's a bit of a sore spot with me."

"Think nothing of it. I know more about war than you think. Less than twenty years ago, we were at war with Mexico back when Texas was a brand new State. This was only a few years after the Alamo." Dewy hung his head. He knew what that meant. Lawrence continued somberly. "I remember what it was like to come home; to try to sleep but not able to quiet the echoes of gunfire and screaming men in my ears. Catherine, God bless her, was wonderful. She helped me heal. You don't have anyone to walk you through it. I only wish to be here for you when you can talk. That's all."

"I appreciate the offer, Lawrence. I do; sincerely." He wasn't sure how Lawrence would react to the idea of Dewy fighting for the Union. He wasn't ready to tell him, and he knew he'd only be here for a few more days.

"Truth is, Dewy. I know. I know which side you fought for." Dewy went to say something, but was stopped by a hand held in the air. "You shouted it out a few nights ago. How the Rebs were on every side. How you had to kill to survive. I know."

Dew hung his head yet again. He wondered if he needed to move on. "Look, if having me - the enemy, so to speak - here is too hard, I can move on. I won't tell Miss Catherine why; I'll just go."

"I figure, at this point, it doesn't matter. It's all over and done with, in my opinion. Both sides suffered great loss. You're one of the lucky ones. You have all your limbs and you're alive." Lawrence said, sympathetically.

"I pray I never met one of your boys in battle. I don't know if I could live with that. I won't find out until I face the Almighty. But, all the same..."

"Andrew." Dewy's full name gained his attention. "I want you to stay as long as you need. You're secret is safe with me. I won't even tell Catherine until after you've moved on. In my mind, and heart, you're as much a son to me as if you'd been a Rebel."

With a half-grin, Dewy replied. "Thank you for your understanding and kindness towards me. I'd better finish here and wash up before Miss Catherine decides to holler at us for missing breakfast." Lawrence laughed as he stood and shook Dewy's hand.

"I want you to know you can come to me with anything, Dewy. The burden you carry is hard and heavy. Not many men can relate to a battle weary heart." Patting his pocket, Lawrence withdrew an envelope. "Before I forget; this came for you yesterday. It's from Comfort, Texas." Nodding, he handed the letter to Dewy and left the barn.

Dewy stared at the envelope for what seemed an eternity. How it ever reached him, he didn't know. He'd been at the Monroe's for three weeks, almost four. He opened it, forgetting the work he had to finish or the breakfast waiting for him.

Dear Dewy,

I received your letter today. I hope this response finds it way to you. I'm glad you are safe. I'm glad you're alive. And so is your Paw. He is not opposed to your homecoming now, though I think the Good Lord has more softening to do in his heart before you arrive.

Philip sends his regards, though he's a bit on the indignant side when it come to your impending return. His countenance changed after I allowed him to read your letter.

I pray, and haven't stopped since the morning you left, for your safe return to us. If you are still in Jackson, I pray you are making plans to return soon. Ellisa sends her regards and is also anxious for your return.

All my love,

Mother

Dewy wiped his face, erasing evidence of the tears that escaped in the short message from home. His Paw was thinking of his return? He was considering welcoming him back? The Lord's wonders truly never did cease, and he was once again overtaken with emotion. Shaking his head, he finished placing feed in the trough and walked to the outside pump to wash up for the morning meal.

The Way Across

With a promise to write as often as possible, Dewy hugged Catherine and Lawrence Monroe one last time before mounting Bess and riding away. Goodbyes had always been difficult at best for Dewy and leaving the Monroes had put a serious damper on his demeanor. They had become close friends, always confident in their Lord and in themselves, and never afraid to rebuke in love; much like his mown parents.

A few days had passed since he'd said farewell and headed west once again. Not too much longer, and he'd be facing the biggest river in the East: The Mississippi. To avoid sinking into a lonely depression, his mind went into planning and plotting how to cross the giant flow. No doubt it would be too deep for Bess to cross on foot. He'd have to find a way. With little money, and not knowing what was accepted in the area, he wasn't sure he could hire a ferry boat. But, no other solutions came to mind off-hand either.

"No sense in borrowing trouble." Dewy said aloud, but mostly to hear a human voice instead of the whinnies and neighs provided by

Bess. He passed another homestead, but kept moving. He wanted to make it as far as possible before sundown. He would stop in the heat of the day under trees and near water, if possible. Bess needed water and rest. She was good about eating the grass nearby and seemed a very low maintenance horse. He urged her into a slow gallop, not wanting to expend her energy too early in the day. Bess complied with his command of two clicks of his tongue and went faster.

A sad song seemed to come from nowhere, and with no one but Bess to listen, Dewy began to sing; slowly and quietly at first, but then louder and with more confidence as the song built in his heart. How he missed evenings on the porch with his brother, Philip, a harmonica, a banjo, and a fire blazing. "Good times," his voice echoed in his head. He continued singing to ward off the melancholy that came with the thought of his brother as he and Bess moved ever closer to the river.

~~~~~

He did have a destination, Philip Montgomery told himself as he ambled away from his small home towards town. He had a small errand to run before heading to his parents' place for a visit. He was worried about how them and the whole "Dewy" situation.

The tune he whistled forced him to remember all those nights during the summer when he and Dewy would entertain themselves, and many of the other youth from the surrounding area, with music, singing, story-telling, and even dancing. Violins and guitars accompanied them every now and again, and the ladies loved to laugh and flirt with the boys under the stars. Their parents were always nearby as proper chaperones for the young ladies, and many a love match began right in the Montgomery's front yard. Those were the days.

Now the bitterness of Dewy's defiance left a bad taste in his mouth, and he spit into the dirt as if doing so could rid him of the memory. He just couldn't get past the final blow: Dewy waving and boarding the train while his Maw cried and anger set onto his Paw's face, causing lines to draw his normally happy countenance into a lasting frown. Then the image of Miss Emma Jenkins crying by herself as her intended and her brother boarded the train with him. He could still smell the acrid smoke from the locomotive and hear the whistle as it took them closer to their deaths. Philip found it hard to believe that those events had taken place more than three years ago. And while Dewy was off playing soldier, this town had refused to breathe in hopes that the native sons would return from war to their loved ones.

Philip released a ragged breath at the vivid memory of what he considered his brother's betrayal: How he'd torn the family asunder by one bold act, hurting his Mother's heart the way he had. And now? Now the boy wanted to come back and make like nothing had happened. How dare he? Had he not yet figured out that his actions had consequences? That he'd hurt everyone he loved and those who loved him? Philip wondered if those thoughts had even crossed his younger brother's mind.

Paying no mind to his whereabouts, Philip was caught off guard when he bumped into someone: Emma Jenkins.

"Beg pardon, Miss Jenkins." He made a slight bow. "I must not have been looking where I was going. Are you harmed?" He asked, reaching for her elbow to steady her from teetering and falling; his former train of thought derailed in the presence of a sweet young lady. She'd been through a tough season recently. His heart immediately went out to her.

"No, Mr. Montgomery. No harm done. How's Dewy?" She asked sincerely, sending him back into his former anger. He had no time to respond. "Ellisa received another letter from him. I just wondered if you or your parents had heard from him as well."

"Thank you for your concern, Miss Jenkins. I don't honestly have any idea. Mother might have heard from him, but he has yet to see fit to send me any messages." Suddenly thinking he sounded too gruff, he readjusted his thinking with a shake of his head. "I apologize for my rude discourse. How are you faring?"

"As well as can be expected, I suppose." Emma shrugged her shoulder and turned her head at her own statement, but did not expound on it.

"If there is anything you or your family has need of, please don't hesitate to ask me. I am at your disposal." He bowed with a smile, kissing her gloved hand, as propriety dictated.

"Thank you ever so much, Mr. Montgomery." Emma blushed as she curtsied. She was not used to attention from the gentlemen as of late, much less handsome ones. After her beau had gone off to war, and then died, she didn't seem to want to speak to any of them. There weren't many in Comfort to speak to as it was. Now Philip was giving her attention, and she wasn't sure how to conduct herself. Panic set in, causing her heart rate to rise, and with a beleaguered excuse, she made a hasty retreat. "I'm afraid I must go. Good day, Mr. Montgomery."

"Good day, Miss Jenkins. Please extend my greetings to your parents." He smiled, waving as she slowly backed away.

"I will." She blushed, turned, and ran like a schoolgirl after meeting a boy she liked. "I'm being so silly." She said to herself as she found her Ma in the Dry Goods Store.

Philip shook his head and chuckled as he continued on towards his destination with a satisfied expression on his face; his errand and former contemplations forgotten. He headed left to the lane that lead out of town towards his father's homestead with Emma Jenkins' lovely, blushing face fresh in his memory.

~~~~~

Dewy had, by midday, made it to the great River, and began looking for a way to cross it. He wandered up and down the nearby road, unable to locate a ferry boat or any other conveyance. He had yet to see any locals who could point him in the right direction. He was unsure what to do.

He led Bess down to the bank, careful not to fall into the swiftly moving water as it gurgled over a large grouping of stones, sending a small spray of water into his face. Dewy's laughter bubbled up from his heart. He ambled back with the horse, eager to secure her and then partake of what little provision he had left. He'd have to catch his food the next time he wanted to eat.

Refreshed after a little rest, Dewy mounted Bess and headed south a bit, hoping to find a means of crossing. The road was dirt, mud, and gravel mixed and was a bit hard on his mare, but they moved on down a ways.

"At last," he muttered when he finally did see a ferry boat crossing. Approaching, he sized up the the miniscule vessel, but decided to ask the elderly man, who was missing teeth when he smiled, about crossing.

"Hello, sir. Do you have room for a horse aboard?" Dewy called out. "I'm prepared to pay well!"

"Sorry, boat's too small. A mile down is another ferry boat, if'n you wanna try that. Otherwise, you're gonna hafta swim!" The old codger laughed.

Dewy waved a silent thank you before nudging Bess on down the road, sticking to the edge of the tree line to save her shoes. Dewy didn't need to add an extra day or two to the journey to shoe the beast.

Arriving at the next crossing, Dewy heaved a deep breath, hoping to get to the other side before dark. This was by far the most difficult part: Finding a way across.

"Say, good man, do you have room for a horse?" Dewy called out as he approached the dock. The wind picked up a bit, blowing a nice breeze through his hair, cooling him a bit from the mid day heat.

The ferry boat worker ignored Dewy as he approached. The bald man with dark skin just kept on scrubbing the deck of his small boat.

Dewy cleared his throat. "Hello! How are you today?" The man said nothing and did not even acknowledge his presence. Dewy tied the horse to the dock post and stepped aboard.

With that gesture, the man stood, looking blankly at him. Without warning, the man stomped on the deck twice, scaring Dewy into jumping back a bit.

A woman ran up from below deck. "What can I do for ya, sir?" She said with a smile; her gray and black hair standing straight out in all directions. "My boat captain be deaf. He cain't hear the wind blowin'. You needin' a ride 'cross?"

"Yes, Ma'am. I was wondering if you had room for my horse." He asked, hat in hand in an effort to appear meek and innocuous. He smiled timidly, praying inside for mercy and grace and a ride across the muddy river.

"Well, lemme aks 'im." With a few crude gestures, the woman conveyed the message. The man shook his head no. He gestured to the woman that the horse was too big, but then shrugged.

"Sorry, sir, but he say no. He think your horse gonna sink our boat." She said, and turned to go back down the ladder she had come up from. Dewy nodded in understanding.

"Beggin' pardon, Ma'am," she giggled when he called her Ma'am; "but, I don't see a long line of customers waitin', and I'm trying to get back to Texas to my Maw and Paw. Could you ask him again? I am a solitary traveler, accepting my horse, of course." She grunted disapprovingly, but caught the boat captain's attention and asked again.

A long moment passed. The man stood, again, eyeing Dewy up and down, and then doing the same to Bess. He held out his hand for a moment and Dewy supposed he meant to ask for payment.

Dewy gave him a note equaling One Dollar. The man's eyes lit up! He nodded and grinned, signaling for Dewy to bring the horse aboard.

"Thank you! Thank you so much!"

"We be leavin' in a bit. You wantin' sumpin' ta eat?"

"Oh, no Ma'am, but thank you. I just ate supper a little while ago."

"Maybe before we make it 'cross, you be eatin'." She laughed a little and went down below. Dewy eyed the man as he went across the boat deck once again to fetch his horse. He almost wanted to ask how long they'd been running the boat, but refrained. The man wouldn't hear him anyway and they may have just been freed recently.

After what felt an eternity, the old woman returned to the top of the boat. She and the man gestured and grunted for several very long minutes before she glanced at Dewy. "Moses say we gon' go 'head, but there's a storm a'brewin'. He say if the boat feel like it gon' go topsy-turvy, the horse will be da firs' to go. Fair 'nough?"

Dewy protested inwardly, but agreed. "I'd say so, but I think we'll do everything we can to prevent that." He laughed awkwardly, but then jumped up from sitting on the boat deck to help the man she called Moses push off from the dock. With a sigh he looked up river and then down.

He was that much closer to home!

The Mighty Mississip

T he wooden craft they called a boat had seen better days. The longer Dewy spent aboard the small conveyance, the more he realized it was a glorified raft and not a ferry. Moses used a giant paddle all in place of a steam engine to help it get across the narrower portion of river. The second "story" of the boat was really a hole in the floor with dilapidated housing surrounding it. No doubt, this was for protection from the weather. Moses also had a small shelter at the bow so he could navigate regardless of condition outdoors. It appeared that this was their home and not just their means of income. The kindly older woman invited Dewy to join her there when the rain started.

"How long have you had your boat?" He asked, hoping it wasn't too personal.

"Oh, twunny years or so." She grinned broadly. "We wuz slaves, but when our massuh died, he din't have nobody who wanted his property. So, we wuz set free by his wife who was never much a friend of slavery. It was touch and go at times, but we managed to stay outta sight. We almost got taken and sold agiyun, but nobuddy wanted no old folks. The Lord seen us through. We ain't seen our chil'ren or granchil'ren for a long time. Now we don't hafta worry so much. We so glad Mistuh Lincoln set us free."

Dewy hoped his shock didn't register on his face. They'd struggled through some rough years, trying to keep their freedom and survive. Sudden pride swelled inside Dewy's heart like a huge wave overtaking the shore: He'd fought for this. He'd fought for Moses and his wife. Dewy turned towards the door, looking at the water, so she wouldn't see the tears flowing down his face unimpeded.

"You alright, Sir?" She asked with concern thick as syrup in her voice.

In a whispered reply, Dewy affirmed.

"What's gotcha so quiet suddenly?" The as yet unnamed elderly woman queried, bringing Dewy out of his reverie.

"It's nothing, Ma'am; just memories and a grateful heart." Dewy had yet to come out of his quiet and pensive mood.

"Was you a soldier?" She asked out of nowhere. "You act like you was, and hold yo'self up higher than men who wasn't."

"Yes, Ma'am. I'm finally returning home. It's been a longer journey than I anticipated, but I'm about halfway there."

The woman smiled, revealing a black hole instead of teeth, forcing a grin from Dewy before her face turned serious and her brow very wrinkled. "Was you a rebel soldier?"

That question straightened him up and caused him to stand almost at attention. He wasn't sure how she'd feel about his loyalties. He answered hesitantly. "No, Ma'am. Not many Southern boys fought for the Union, but I was one of them." Ruth then did the most unexpected thing: She hugged Dewy.

"I be so glad to hear that, and happy to hepp you get a little further along. Name's Ruth (which came out Rufth due her lack of teeth)."

"I'm glad to meet you, Ruth." The older woman giggled when he took her hand and kissed it like she were a society lady. "I'm Andrew." She smiled again, but said nothing more, and went about her duties.

Turning back to his own inner thoughts, he eyed the clouds from the door, noticing their darkening in conjunction with the swift movement of the water. It appeared to be churning almost as they slowly passed over it.

Two very hard stomps on the upper deck ricocheted off the walls in the lower deck. Dewy moved up the last two steps quickly so Miss Ruth could see what Moses wanted. Dewy watched, riveted by their silent conversation. He realized he was eavesdropping on them in a way. He turned to the side where Bess was standing, growing agitated by the impending storm. Dewy wondered if that was the subject of their conversation. He guessed they were close to halfway across.

He pet his horse for a minute before going back to the inside room. He grabbed an apple from his bag and all but sprinted up the stairs back to Bess. "Here ya go, girl." He fed her the red treat all the while stroking her neck and mane. Dewy could sense when Miss Ruth had finished talking to her husband and heard her cross the small deck to stand behind him. He turned when she began speaking to him.

"Moses say yo horse spookin' could tip the boat. He trying to get us acrossed fast as he can, but the wind and the water is workin' against him. You strong; you can hepp him, right?" Dewy didn't answer immediately, but continued soothing Bess, who was calming despite the weather's turn for the worse. How could he say no? The man had to be ten years older than his grandfather and was moving this vessel alone. Did he have another paddle, or was he just too tired to continue to fight the river? Dewy's questions would go unanswered.

With a nod of his head, he agreed. "She's calming now. I'll put a blanket over her so she isn't so scared. I'm glad to help, but Moses will have to show me what to do. And how do I talk to him?"

"He sees what you say. Talk slow-like and he answer you with grunts and nods and pointing. Stomp twice if you need my hepp. Thank you." Ruth patted his shoulder before taking his hand in both of hers and leading him over to Moses. "He gots another paddle for ya. You gone hafta stand in the rain. You can paddle next to your horse, if'n you wanna. That ways you know she okay, too."

"No problem, Ma'am. I can stand by Bess."

"Thank ya." She said with a little tuck of her chin.

"My pleasure." Ruth ran back into her tiny abode and left the men to work.

The rain seemed to dump from the sky at that moment, soaking Dewy, Moses, and poor Bess. She seemed to ride the storm out unless it thundered or lightning flashed. Moses kept a wary eye on the large animal. Dewy only stopped paddling to stroke her until she calmed, and then went back to his task.

Memories seemed to assault him as he struggled against the strong current with the paddle; memories of marching in the rain, finding their next encampment sight, setting up gear and finding a way to eat cold beans while hoping for their gear to dry. Torrential downpours happened in spring and summer in the South, making a soldier's life difficult at times. The animals didn't like to be outdoors, and, unless a barn was nearby, they were out in the elements. One particular day in early summer stood out.

"Montgomery! Go get the Captain's horse to shelter." Dewy looked around. Nothing for a long stretch in any direction seemed to jump out at him. The fields must've spanned a mile in every direction: nothing but white cotton balls stood to one side across the dirt road. The wind picked up, and the clouds darkened as if on cue from the Confederate President to halt the Northern advance.

Dewy saluted the captain, took the reins, and headed the horse toward a large grouping of Magnolia trees whose fragrant white blossoms reminded him of his mother and a pretty girl. He tied the horse and went back for other animals, but was halted by the downpour. He waited with the agitated horse, petting it's back and sides in attempt to keep it from injuring him in its fright.

Hours passed before the storm let up. It was dark before the clouds were completely gone, leaving a muddy, wet mess of an encampment. Despite the shelter from the grove of magnolias, Dewy was soaked to the bone and had no lantern to see his way back to where he'd left his gear. His shelter wasn't even set up yet. He was sure everything was completely sopping inside his pack anyway. If he'd heard correctly, they'd be there a few days, so hopefully, God willing, tomorrow's sunshine would dry his things out . Sleeping with a horse for a companion was on his list of things to do, but Dewy sat against the tree and let fatigue overtake him.

He sat there, cold, wet, and half asleep for two hours longer when footsteps from behind had him on his guard, suddenly wide awake. He reached for his side arm and keeping his hand there. "Who goes there? Identify yourself!" He said forcefully, unwilling to risk the Captain's horse for any reason. God forbid it was Confederate spies or an ambush. He didn't have any way to signal an attack from where he slept. When there was no immediate answer, he drew his sidearm, looking to see if he could find the source of the footsteps.

"I said who goes there?" Dewy thought for sure the horse would get loud, waking the camp and causing the Officers awaken, cranky, before dawn. That would cause ill feelings for Dewy from his fellow Enlisted men. Dewy didn't need that kind of attention.

He cocked his pistol when he heard a familiar voice whisper back.

"It's me: Clem!" Dewy sighed in relief. "I was, you know, getting some relief. Need a lantern to get back?"

"I figured I'd stay with old Doyle here, as I don't even have my shelter set up. I'm thinking everything is wet. Pointless to set up in the dark, don'tcha think?"

"I set it up for ya, but your right. It's all wet. I put your clothes across your cot so they can dry some. You should be able to sleep dry tomorrow. Want me to stay and keep ya company? I'm a little more conversational than old Doyle here."

Dewy let out a quiet laugh. "That you are, Clem. I'm guessing we only have a couple hours 'til dawn. What was for dinner?"

"Cold beans and bread. What we had that was salvageable in our packs. Man, I'm glad this ain't winter time. We'd be freezing by now."

"You're spot on there, Clem. I tell ya, nights like this, I sure miss home. I reckon I'm not the only one, but it seems that way sometimes. I wonder about Ellisa. I know you wonder how Anna Beth's faring."

"I miss that girl something awful, Dewy. I wish I'd of married her before I left. Sometimes I think I won't make it back to her." Clem choked on the last few words, and Dewy patted his shoulder.

"Ya can't go thinkin' like that. At least your girl still wants you. I am to make it home just to prove to her I love her, and pray every day until I do that she takes me back."

The two best friends talked until they heard the rooster crow in the distance.

Dewy shook his head to dislodge the memory from his mind's eye. He missed his best friend more than words could ever express. The rain continued to pour over him like a waterfall. The river was angry; at whom, Dewy wasn't sure. Maybe it was angry at the storm for causing such turmoil, or at the man and the boat for trying to cross during the deluge.

An unusually large wave swept up the side of the boat, splashing Dewy and Bess and rocking the boat until it listed just a bit toward the starboard side, causing a strangled sound from the boat's captain, and a scream from Miss Ruth down in the hull.

Dewy pushed Bess towards the edge of the boat, all the while holding her rope. He did not plan to send her over. On the contrary, he hoped her weight would right the boat.

And it did.

Just in time.

The horse neighed at Dewy, as if to say she were upset with him for scaring her. He patted her mane and neck, whispering kind apologies to her as if she were a human.

Before long, the storm had passed and Moses was docking his boat on the other shore with relief that the horse hadn't cost him his boat. At least, that's what it seemed like he was saying as he gestured frantically to Ruth.

"Moses say he gone build a raff to pull behind the boat for horses. He thank ya for ya hepp. He don't think the boat woulda made it if'n you hadn't been on board today." Ruth explained as Dewy led Bess off to the side under some trees. "He say to make sho you stay n' eat wif us befoe you head on down the road."

"I'm already indebted to you allowing us to cross with you. I'd be glad to break bread with you both."

The two men built a fire while Ruth prepared what food they had. The food was blessed, and the three kept company long into the night before turning in. Dawn would come soon enough, and he'd be on his way.

This journey was coming to a swift end. For the moment, Dewy decided to enjoy the company while he had it.

Looking Down the Road

"Have you heard from the wayward boy lately?" Gaius Montgomery asked his bride over breakfast. He still considered Tilly his bride even though they'd been married for nearly thirty years. The love grew with every year. They'd been arranged, but soon found that a love had grown between them and by the time they were wed, Gaius could not imagine life without her.

"I was going to check today. He's been writing to Miss Townsend as well, hoping to salvage what they had before he left. I believe he's thinking of returning here. Gaius, I want my son to come home." She paused, eyeing his expression, which was blank. "Are you willing to allow him back?"

"I can't say either way right now, Tilly. I've been doing much praying about the boy. I'm thankful he survived. I have to be honest with you, though. It's hard to forgive him. He hurt you. He wounded my heart too, but no one makes my bride cry. If he knew how you wept; how much you'd prayed... I find it difficult to let that go."

"Even our Lord forgave, Gaius, and while he was dying. You have to forgive. It only hurts you, causing bitterness to lodge itself deep in the cracks of your heart, to the point where you won't, forgive. Gaius, our son is alive. Look around at the devastation this war has caused and tell me you'd rather he be dead."

"You know that's not how I feel..." He replied a little too loudly, pounding the table with his fist. Anxiety stirred his features, ocean tempests raged in his deep blue eyes.

Tilly's permanently soft response banked his anguish. "I know. But think about the Jenkins. They never get to see Clem's face again. They never get to see him marry or hold his children. We're blessed. There's so much we have to be grateful for, and the fact that Dewy is alive ought to cause you to hit your knees in thanksgiving for it."

"What about Mary? Where's she? Her husband went off to war too and now she's raising three young'uns without him. If it weren't for his family, she might not have anything. How's that a blessing?"

"She has their children and God saw fit to give her a good family to help her. And she has us. I help every chance I get. I agree that the war was wrong, but let's not change the subject. We're talking about Dewy coming home. Joseph is gone. Clem is gone. Half the people in Comfort have lost their men. We have our boy and he wants to make it right. Gaius John Montgomery..." His full name from Tilly's beautiful mouth gave him pause. Her eyes, barely holding the tears at bay, begged him to see reason and allow their boy to come home.

"Alright, Tilly, I'll think on it." Standing, he pulled her to him, circling her waist with one arm while the other gently put her head on his shoulder. The dam holding her salty tears burst against him, wetting his shirt.

~~~~~

After a brief rest for both man and beast, Dewy packed his gear and saddled up. He had to head south and west as he aimed for home.

"Home. Do I even have one to go back to?" He questioned out loud, while walking his horse. He'd written another letter to his mother, telling her all of the goings-on in his travels. He remembered fondly the people who'd helped him, and prayed for those who didn't, or couldn't help, along the way. A letter to the Monroes was in order just as soon as he was settled in Comfort again. He still didn't know where that would be. So many questions continued to plague his thoughts.

He urged Bess into a trot and rode that way for half a day before stopping. Louisiana was hot and humid. He'd have to rest and water her much more often so she could keep moving. Horses were meant to ride, but not so much that they too fell from the heat.

The pungent smell of his horse's sweat caused his first battle to race before his eyes.

They sprinted past him as the Cavalry charged. The drums and bugles sounded, men sprinted away from him towards the men in gray.

Dewy stood frozen in fear. All of eighteen years old, and he was fighting for his life. Clem passed him, not stopping. Dewy knew he had to move. He didn't want a bullet to find him an easy target because he stood stationary. He aimed his weapon, and started running for the enemy.

A shout came as a man fell in front of Dewy. He watched the man writhing in pain, holding his arm. He wasn't dying, so Dewy moved forward. Another man, this one on horseback, dropped backwards, the horse bucked and charged in fear as his rider went askew in the saddle. The man's boot caught in the stirrup, not allowing the horse to rid itself of its corpse-rider. His dead body dragged as the horse continued to run until a bullet went through the animal's heart. Both horse and rider fell to the earth, dust kicking up around them as the horse landed on its soldier. Dewy had to keep going. He wasn't the medic and the gray uniforms kept shooting at him. He stopped to reload, kneeling not too far from Clem.

"You alright, Montgomery?"

"Yep. How 'bout you?"

"I'm fine, but this is one bloody mess." Reloaded, Clem jumped up and continued running, Dewy not far behind.

Countless hours passed in the same way, until finally they were told to fall back.

"We're retreating? What? Why?" He glanced in his pouch, realizing his ammunition had all been spent. He ran back across the many acres to the unit encampment, somewhat thankful for the reprieve.

"We made it out alive, Dewy." Clem hollered as they moved away from the formation a while later.

"We lived to fight another day. God is with us, I'd say."

"Not with everyone. Too many blue uniforms are on that field. Let's see if the medics need help." They drank a long time from their canteens, emptying them, before leaving their weapons in their tents and moving on to the hospital tent.

Dewy looked around him, expecting to view a sea of dead and wounded all over the ground. Recognizing it as a memory, he said another silent thank you to the Almighty.

He steered Bess to the trough as he rode into a small town. She needed a rest, and he needed to eat as well. He wondered how far he'd ridden. He was growing weary of traveling, and ready to see his mother, and the feeling intensified when he thought of Ellisa.

He had been preparing land to build a house, a cabin really, for them when the war started. Now, he wondered if his father would even allow him to work as a farm hand.

An idea sprang to mind: He'd ask to work for his keep, sleep in the barn, and when he had enough money, he'd buy land and build his home. Maybe his father would agree to that. He smiled as he bit into his apple.

~~~~~

Tilly went on to town with her buggy to check on their daughter, Mary, and to speak with Ellisa Townsend. She was most curious to know if the sweet girl had received any more missives from Dewy.

She continued praying for her husband all the way down the lane. He had to realize what a deep blessing he really had, knowing his son lived. Her heart cried to her Lord, longing for Gaius to understand what had been so blatantly obvious to her: Dewy and Gaius must make amends if they wanted to live a happy life. A separation of this magnitude could rend a family in two forever. That cost was one Tilly knew she could not afford.

Mary met her mother, Tilly, at the front door, smiling.

"What brings you today, Ma?" She asked, shushing her youngest boy in her arms. Her four year old daughter was running behind the older boy, playing tag in the yard.

"I thought to check on you. I came to town to see if Dewy had sent another letter."

"You've received letters from Dewy? Oh, how wonderful. Where is he?"

"Last I heard, Mary, he was in Mississippi. He stayed a few weeks there to help a farmer. I haven't received another letter since then. Hopefully all is well. How are you?"

"Oh, Ma, some days are better than others. I have considered moving out West. Men working there are looking for brides. The children and I would have support. Not to worry, though. It will be a long while before I act on that thought. I miss Joseph too much as it is."

"I cannot imagine how difficult this is for you. Of course, you and the children are always welcome to live with us. We've plenty of room, and the little ones would be good for your Pa. He needs some joy in his life." Tilly smiled wistfully.

"Thanks, Ma. We're very blessed to have a home, and Joseph had income saved, so for now, we have provisions. Besides, I've heard rumors about Comfort building a small schoolhouse. I could teach there. The children and I are in God's hands. We'll be fine."

Mary, more at peace than Tilly had first thought, went in to put little Jacob in his bed. Tilly called to Joshua and Martha to come to the porch. When they approached, she handed each one a nickel. "Don't tell your Mamma where it came from, okay? Here, Martha, hold one for Jacob, and next time you go to the General Store, buy yourselves some licorice." Tilly smiled at her beautiful grandchildren. "Hush now. You mustn't let on that you have a little spending money. It's a gift from Grandmamma and Grandpapa, okay?"

"Yes, Grandmamma, we'll keep quiet about it." They said in unison. They went into the house quietly and put their new treasures under their pillows, careful not to wake Jacob.

"Ma, you really mustn't spoil the children so. Their teeth will fall out of their mouths with so much licorice." Mary chided, shaking her head and chuckling as she walked out. "Do you want to come in for some lemonade?"

"No, I must be getting on to town. Here. This is for you. Go buy some fabric for a new dress. You need to treat yourself now and again. I know it's been months, but I still worry over you." Tilly hugged her daughter. "And I won't take no for an answer."

Mary dabbed her eyes with the corner of her apron and then hugged her mother close. "You're so good to us, Ma. Thanks. We're really okay. I know Joseph is with the Lord, and I know that we'll meet again. I miss him so, especially at night when the children are sleeping. That's when we had our conversations."

"Your Pa and I are the same way. God will bring you someone when it's time, if that's what you want. I need to get along. I have much to do and the day's wasting away." Tilly hugged Mary goodbye, and climbed back onto her wagon, steering towards town.

~~~~~

He'd made his decision. Comfortable with it, because he never second guessed himself, Gaius stood on his porch, staring down the road. He hadn't moved since Tilly left for town. Pulling out his loose tobacco, he stuffed the shredded leaves into his pipe, puffing to light it. He drew a deep breath, exhaled the white smoke, and sat on the porch swing.

And there he'd watch for Dewy to come down the road.

He'd watch, and he'd wait.

And Yet So Far...

Dewy finally stopped at dusk. He had asked permission to sleep in a barn and for his horse to graze. The lady of the house brought him food and coffee. The man of the house was a bit apprehensive, but eventually allowed him to stay. Dewy left a small thank you in the form of a dollar, and rode away before dawn. If he'd figured correctly, he had about three days more until he reached Texas. It felt like an eternity.

Unless, of course, he found the train.

According to the kind folks, he could even board Bess in the cargo hold and ride clear from Alexandria all the way to Houston. Then, they'd given him a train voucher, saying it had been purchased for their cousin, but the cousin had fought and died, like so many others, and now it was going to waste.

Dewy smiled as he pushed Bess into a gallop, promising to slow her down a little as the sun grew warmer. He hoped to make it in time to board. That would cut his trip by almost a full week. He could be home in those same three days.

"Gee-up." He urged Bess on, seeing home on the horizon.

~~~~~

Ellisa opened another letter from Dewy. She was beginning to entertain the idea of his homecoming; the very thought brought a broad grin to her features.

Dearest Ellisa,

As I travel across the southern United States, I am astonished at the devastation we have caused. It seems every story ends the same: "The Union Army did damage, our son, or sons, died in a battle." I find it almost too great a pain to bear.

I left the farm of the Monroes and am headed toward Louisiana. I am hoping to make my arrival in Comfort near Thanksgiving, but one can never know for sure.

I pray this finds you well, and I hope beyond words that you will once again accept me. Leaving you was inevitable as far as things of war, but my heart stayed in Comfort with you. I've thought of you endlessly, imagining our discussions after I return. I replay events we shared and long ago conversations.

Be blessed, sweet Ellisa. I will see you face to face again very soon.

Yours forever,

Andrew "Dewy" Montgomery

Her heart swelled with a sudden longing for Dewy to be home. Ellisa could no longer deny her love for him, or the fact that she needed him by her side. Now she had to pray and pray hard for the Lord, and Dewy, to forgive her the bitterness and anger she felt towards him while he was away.

~~~~~

Philip Montgomery found ways to continue "accidentally" meeting up with Emma Jenkins. He thought the young woman kind, and she was beautiful as well. He took a deep breath as he dressed for Sunday services. He would meet his mother and father, and they, no doubt, planned to have him over for dinner afterwards. The harvest was almost in completely, and they would celebrate Thanksgiving in a few days.

He thought of Dewy and wondered how he would spend the day, and if he would even eat. He still resented his brother and wasn't sure he could fathom what a homecoming would be like, but concern welled up in his being nonetheless for his younger sibling.

Shaking his head, he snorted. "As if I actually felt sorry for the boy. I won't be so welcoming. I've had to see the pain and damage he's caused first hand." He only spoke aloud to keep his thinking from changing like it seemed his father's had. "Maybe Miss Jenkins will want to go for a walk after service."

Whistling a lively tune to dissipate the loneliness that suddenly surrounded him, Philip went on foot towards the main part of town. Dewy was once again in the back of his mind. If Philip had his way, Dewy would remain there.

~~~~~

Dewy slowed his horse at another watery crossing. It was a small creek when compared to the Mississippi, but Bess would be almost up to her girth in water. He'd direct her down the riverbed a ways to find a more shallow depth.

A lone sound echoed in the quiet; a sound he'd longed to hear since he began this journey so many weeks before. Edging Bess into a gallop towards it, Dewy brought her up short as the steam engine powered passed them. She wasn't too fond of the noise and reared up, but Dewy's excitement could not be contained.

In one swift movement, he pulled her reins a bit to the right, tapping her flank with his heel to urge her faster. He rode and tried to keep up with the locomotive until it was out of sight.

"Thanks be unto God, I found the rails. Now to home, Bess! Now to home!"

He settled her for a while, to allow her to drink, before heading west once again. Dewy had made up his mind he would not stop until he found a way to board a train. While she nibbled at the grass, he decided to take out his harmonica. He hadn't felt the want to do that in quite some time, and his joy overflowed. He'd be home in less than three days.

His mind wandered back to another day during the war. A day he'd just as soon forget if he could.

Heart pounding, Dewy looked around for Clem. They'd been battle buddies since the first skirmish; really, since they could both walk. He couldn't remember a day without his best friend. Now, he was missing. Bodies, once again, lay everywhere; some still moving, some crying out, and some staring with that glassy-eyed look that said the soul had departed. Where was Clem?

Dewy set to finding him. "Jenkins! Corporal Jenkins!" He looked, careful not to dishonor the fallen by stepping on them. He had to stop more times than he could count and wait for medics He became one of the "the finders of the living" for that day. There were always men out on the battle field, looking for them: the injured, bleeding, or maybe under a corpse for protection against the enemy.

"Jenkins! Corporal Clem Jenkins!" He continued to shout as he waved the cot-bearers to yet another injured man.

"I-I h-h-hope ya find 'im." The man said, clutching his side in a futile attempt to stay the bleeding coming from it. Dewy wouldn't be surprised if that one died in surgery for the amount he'd lost.

"Thank you. God be with you, brother." He said that to everyone he found.

"Over here." Dewy heard first then looked in the direction of the voice. "He's over here." Another Private waved at him like a ship found after days adrift on the ocean.

Dewy ran.

Dewy ran so fast and so hard, sweat poured down his face despite the cool temperature of that fall afternoon.

Out of breath to the point of bending over to recuperate, he arrived at his fallen friend's side. Before he could ask where and how he was hurt, Clem began to tell him.

"My leg. A round hit me hard. It's deep. Dewy, I can't stop the blood, not even tying it with a strip from my shirt."

Dewy breathed, bending low to examine the mangled pieces left of his friend's upper thigh. He was gonna lose his leg.

Dewy, praying for forgiveness, lied to his best friend. "Everything's gonna be okay. We're gonna get you to the hospital and get it fixed up."

"Dewy, I'm no ignoramus. I know I'm gonna lose it. Do you think Anna Beth will still want me with a leg missing?"

"I'm sure she loves you with or without it, Clem. Now, go get fixed up so you can see her again." Dewy called to him as they hoisted him atop the stretcher and ran for the hospital wagon that would take him into surgery.

That was the last time he saw his best friend alive.

An unchecked tear slid down his cheek. Dewy wished so many times he's said more, or told Clem how much of a brother he really was to him. The funeral was a mass funeral with so many others, and Dewy wished they'd had a private one for his friend. He realized he'd be retelling that tale to the Jenkins family in a very short time. Maybe someday he could go back with the Jenkins family to Clem's grave; pay the respects he deserved. What could one put on such a little stone to honor all that his best friend had done for him?

Shaking his head to clear his reverie, he mounted his horse and spurred her on towards what he hoped would be a nearby train depot. He was so close to home, he could feel the Texas wind at his face. "And yet, I am so far away." Bess's ears perked at his voice as he rode upon a depot. "So far away."

Journey's End

"Where'r'ya headin', son?" The station manager asked Dewy while chewing his tobacco. His beard and wire-rimmed glasses made him look ten years older than Dewy's Paw.

"I'm headin' home to Texas. I've been walking since summer started and I'm almost there. In fact, this train station was heaven-sent. I might otherwise have another week on my mare over yonder."

"Are you returning from the War?" The man asked with a gleam in his eye. "I have a brother who fought. He's alive, but missin' his arm and walkin' with a limp. He's a couple decades my junior, mind you. My Pop married twice. I'm from the first marriage, he's from the second. But, we're glad he's a-livin', for sure."

"As a matter of fact, I am. I was in Georgia at the last." Dewy's far-away look returned. The memories weren't as constant as they were at the start of his voyage, but they still always stood at the ready to remind him of the horrors and pains associated with fighting and killing.

"Welp, I tell ya what ... Your ticket here is on me. We'll getcha home for Thanksgiving. It's this week, ya know. I betcha your maw will be right pleased to lay eyes on you." He smiled broadly, turning to spit in his spittoon while awaiting Dewy's answer.

"I already have a ticket, but thanks just the same."

"I guess that's settled."

"My horse. Is there a car for her?"

"With hay and water. She's free too. Did you ride mounted during the War?"

"No, sir, I did not. She's been a gentle, steady companion for me, though." Dewy lifted his cheek in a one-sided grin.

"Train should be here in about three hours. You hungry? I'm certain the wife has somethin' to spare for a travelin' man. Bring your mare, too. She can have hay and water in the back while we wait."

Three hours was a long time to wait in Dewy's mind. He'd become a very patient man, but when food was offered, he knew better than to decline it.

"I reckon that sounds right perfect, sir. Thank you." He followed the station attendant, walking next to Bess with reins in hand.

~~~~~

Those several hours passed quickly with conversation, laughter, and too much food. Dewy had been welcomed and accepted, but could not still the anxious feelings that crowded his heart when he remembered he was almost home.

Before he could say anything, his host announced: "I'd say it's 'bout time to get on back to that station. The locomotive should be arriving within the hour."

"Thank you, Ma'am, for your hospitality. I appreciate the meal, and your company." He kissed her hand and bowed before finding his hat and walking towards the front door.

"Young man, Yankee or Reb, you are most welcome anytime you find yourself coming through. It was a pleasure. Let me get a small package of food for you before you leave." The kind woman insisted on giving him bread, cheese, cookies, and anything else she could put into the small kerchief she'd tied with a string. It seemed to bulge at odd angles from the amount of food-stuffs she had provided. Patting his shoulder, she smiled. "There. That should have you set at least for today." She gave him an impromptu hug before sending her husband and Dewy on their way.

He led Bess back to the train depot, following the station manager, in silence. Many thoughts crossed his mind, so clear he could see them.

Ellisa. Would she welcome him with open arms again? Or would a cold shoulder and tear-filled eyes greet him upon his return.

Ma. He knew in his heart she would weep when they met again, and yet it comforted him to know someone had prayed for him all this time.

Pa. Could he welcome his son home? Or would Dewy get the steel-blue gaze and silence. Too many nights, he'd dreamt of his father turning his head away and pointing to the road.

Even Philip. He hadn't thought Philip would want to hear from him, but now he felt a bit of remorse for not corresponding with his brother. They were so close. He prayed silently that they could be again someday.

The sharp whistle broke the silence as they reached the depot platform. He watched in awe as the smoke rose against the blue sky and the black engine slowed to a stop in front of him.

"This here train will take you all the way to San Antonio. Take care of yourself, young man. You are always welcome here, as my wife stated earlier, even if you did fight for the Yanks. You're a Southern boy just the same, and alive at that. I could tell by his face that my brother was glad to have another soldier about."

"It was my pleasure to be in your family's company today. I am truly grateful for your kind hospitality. You've made me feel most welcome, and like I was already home."

Dewy was cut short by the conductor's announcement: "All aboard!" He bid the man farewell, handed Bess off to the livery hand and boarded the train.

As it pulled off, he could see the man waving, and he returned the gesture in kind. His thoughts retraced the conversation held with the man's brother about the war.

"I saw too many people die, if'n you ask me, from both sides of the fight. People I knew and loved lost their lives. To say an event such as that is horrendous doesn't do justice to the unspeakable things that went on there. Where were you stationed?"

"We moved quite a bit. We started in Virginia, and then went on to North Carolina, Kentucky, Tennessee, and Georgia over the span of three years. I didn't join up until 1862. And you?"

"I can honestly say we fought in so many places, I don't' remember 'em all. I was mostly in Georgia, but we headed back west, fighting off the Yanks in Mississippi, where I broke my leg. We even fought right here in Lou-siana. We won at Palmito Ranch in Texas. That's where I lost my arm. Well, where I was shot in the arm, and all of that. I can't say any of it was good. I can only say we did what we thunk was right."

Dewy nodded and remained silent a moment before saying: "I believe that was every man's intent. My father was, and I imagine still is to some degree, dead set against that War. He said men aren't supposed to kill one another." Dewy went on to tell them his story and how he was heading back without knowing what would happen when he arrived home.

"Son, I believe the Good Lord will work it all out for you. He hears your heart's cry." The woman exhorted him and even prayed with him during the meal that his father's heart would soften.

The countryside passed in a blur of greens, browns, and grays as he smiled at the memory of the fine folks with whom he'd spent his afternoon. He didn't even ask their names, but he would not forget them or their kind nature.

His mind drifted back to Ellisa. He smiled at the thought of her while highlights of their teen years ran wild in his memory. He truly missed her company and the feel of her delicate hand as he held it in his. He missed her soprano voice singing in church, and whispering in his ear a secret for him that she wanted no one else to hear.

~~~~~

The night was over quickly, and he heard someone say they'd crossed the Louisiana State Line into Texas, and then he drifted back to sleep for several more hours.

The giant black train slowed to a stop just as the sun was coming up over the eastern horizon. Dewy jerked awake as the train jolted and came to a stop. Oranges, yellows, blues, and purples dominated the Texas sky in breathtaking hues.

Texas. The word made something swell in his chest.

Was it pride? Perhaps.

Love? Maybe.

Home? Certainly.

He was surprised at the speed of the train. What would normally take days was now over in a matter of hours. He had been certain it would take more than three days on horseback. With the speed of the engine, he now figured a new arrival: No later than the next morning. He would be home for Thanksgiving.

And that was something for which he was truly thankful!

An Answered Prayer

As he fired his gun, killing the goose they'd have for Thanksgiving dinner, only one thought stuck in Gaius Montgomery's mind: Dewy's seat would once again be empty. He'd hoped the boy would've return by now. His last letter greeted them, explaining he was in Louisiana and that he was on horseback. Maybe the boy, if he was still alive, would make it before November, but with that being only two days away, he didn't want to give the idea any merit.

"What's on your mind dear?" Tilly came outside in her work dress and shawl when she saw he had a goose by the neck, ready to clean.

"I was praying Dewy would have made it home by now." He said as he raised his axe to begin the butchering. The sun was just peeking over the horizon. "I suppose we can wait and see if he makes it back before Christmas."

"Gaius, I wish you'd perk up a bit. I don't like seeing you so morose and introspective." Tilly whispered as she watched him prepare the goose.

"I was too hard on the lad." He admitted.

Never one to mince words, Tilly responded in her quiet manner. "Yes, you were, but living in the past won't change the present. If you've asked the Almighty to forgive you, then He already has. All you have to do now is make it right with our son. If his letters were any indication, he's remorseful as well." With a sigh to restrain the tears that tugged at the corner of her eye, Tilly changed the subject. "The girls are coming with the children in a bit. I'd like to get that goose on early so we can eat this afternoon. I'm proud of you, Gaius." She kissed his cheek and went back inside.

Her prayers had been answered, even if Dewy didn't arrive home in time for Thanksgiving.

~~~~~

Philip knocked on the door of the Jenkins' home. He wanted a word with Emma. The past month or so, he'd come to really care for her. He'd learned of her wounded heart firsthand, and made strides to comfort her in her grief. Now, he wanted to court her, but wasn't sure if she would accept.

"Why, hello Philip! What a surprise?" Mrs. Jenkins, in her baking apron, answered the door.

"Hello, Mrs. Jenkins! I came to visit on my way home for the Thanksgiving meal. Is Emma available?" He asked politely, dreaming on the petite woman and her sweet temperament.

He feared the answer even as Mary Jenkins shook her head. "She's in no state to receive company." Mary Jenkins knew all too well the reasons: Clem and Joseph. Mary fought her own emotions, while plastering a pleasant smile to her visage.

"Do convey my heartfelt condolences and sympathies. I'm sure this is a difficult day for the entire family. How thoughtless…"

"Mr. Montgomery!" Emma's voice interrupted his apology. At her shaky voice, his head snapped up to view her at the top of the stairwell. "I'm so glad you came."

He thought he was seeing a vision of an angel as she stood there. She seemed to float as she came down.

"Very well, then. I will continue my baking if you are able to entertain for a while. I'll bring out some lemonade and cookies." Mary walked back to her kitchen, unsure whether to be distracted by the unexpected caller or happy for her daughter.

"I was just on my way to Ma and Pa's for the Thanksgiving meal and thought I'd stop by to see to your welfare." He smiled when he met her at the base of the stairs, offered his arm, and led her to the parlor where they were in view. "How are you fairing today?"

"This is a most difficult day for our family. We all miss Clem so much, and Joseph, too. His mother and father stopped by only last evening to see about us. Oh, Philip. I sometimes wonder…" She sniffed, bowed her head, and wiped the tears with her handkerchief. He patted her other hand, offering silent support. "I apologize."

Philip decided to wait on the question of courting. Maybe she'd be better suited to the idea next spring or summer, after she'd had a year to mourn them both properly.

His unspoken question hung between them for a moment before she took his hand and looked directly into his eyes: "Yes, I do want you to court me." Her whispered announcement left the man gaping in awe at how well she knew his mind. "Mourning periods are for old people. If I've learned one thing from sending Joseph off to war, it's that love is unending, but the ones who matter most are those right here with us," she pat his hand, "and that life continues despite our heartaches. I will always care for him, but that won't bring him out of the ground. You matter to me, Philip Montgomery."

"How did you..." He stammered, still bewildered at her knowledge.

Emma cut him off mid-sentence. "Philip, I never would've thought that I could want another man after Joseph went off and then died, but now..." Philip took his turn to stop her short, but this time it was with a brief kiss.

"I'll talk to your father soon, sweet Emma."

The couple spent a few more moments enjoying one another before Philip said his goodbyes with promises to visit again soon. He flipped his top hat onto his head, turned and blew a kiss to Emma before waving and walking out. Emma stood in the doorway, a sweet blush covering her face, waving for a long moment before going inside to help her mother.

~~~~~

The stopping jolt caused Dewy to stir and look outside. Familiar buildings greeted him and he felt his heart and stomach jump. He'd taken a day to slow down in Houston before continuing on to Comfort. His nerves hadn't let him get on that last train; his emotions too raw to begin the final ride. He'd found a place to rest, taking Bess along for a ride on the outskirts of the city to stretch and graze.

Now, he was finally arriving early on Thursday morning. His mother and father would surely be surrounded soon by Philip, Mary, Emma and their grandchildren as well. Maybe they wouldn't even miss him.

He hoped against hope that dear, sweet Ellisa was surrounded as well by her loved ones.

His thoughts then turned to the Jenkins family. He'd stop there first to give them Clem's personal effects that he managed to acquire after his friend's burial.

He wondered if anyone from the small Texas town of Comfort would even recognize him. He was no longer a fresh faced, wide-eyed, hopeful boy, but a man seasoned by life, death, and war. He was scruffy, rugged, and stinky after traveling, but such was life.

He prayed his family would let him in the yard.

~~~~~

Another knock on the door sent Emma scattering to answer while her mother finished the stuffing.

"Hello! May I help you?" She asked the bearded stranger at her front door. His eyes looked familiar, but she couldn't quite place him.

Her puzzled demeanor caused a chuckle from the man. "Hi, Emma. It's me! Dewy?" A scream pierced the air, followed by the petite girl's arms around his neck.

Mary Jenkins came running from the kitchen, worry shadowing her face. "Emma? What is..?" She stopped short, realizing her daughter's arms were around a man's neck and she was crying. Only a moment later, she realized who Emma was embracing. "Dewy! How we've prayed for you. I'll go fetch Douglas. He'll want to shake your hand."

"I'm going to do more than that." Douglas boomed while hastening across the house to welcome him. "Come here, son, and let me look at you!" He embraced Dewy for a long moment before bringing him into the parlor where Philip and Emma had been just a short hour before.

"I'll not be able to stay long. I'd like to get to the family soon. I brought you Clem's effects." He let that phrase hang in the air while he opened his bag to retrieve them: A daguerreotype of Mary and another of Emma, a small knife with Douglas's name engraved on it, and Clem's Bible. He gave each item to Mary Jenkins before retrieving the next. As expected, a torrent of tears greeted each item in turn. Dewy sat silently, fighting his own emotional outpouring. He had already spent many months weeping in private for his friend. The loss was no less raw now than it had been all those months ago.

"Thank you, Dewy, for bringing Clem's things back to us." Douglas hugged Dewy again as he stood, readying to leave.

"I was glad to do it. He would've done the same for me. There is still much to tell you. I will visit again soon. I need to get on while we still have day light, and I still have another stop before home."

He winked at Emma, who immediately beamed at him. She already knew where he was going, but voiced the question anyway. "Ellisa?" She prayed Ellisa would be as openhearted.

"Of course. I hope she'll be happy to see me."

"Oh, she will be very glad to see you. You look so different, she may not recognize you." She giggled, hugged Dewy again and watched a second Montgomery leave her home in a matter of hours. Philip would be so surprised. Emma refused to bring him up. They had to do their own mending.

~~~~~

Abel Townsend spent the afternoon outside on his front porch. He'd already done all he could to help his wife, Lois, prepare for the meal. Their children were all coming over and the places had been set.

Ellisa, he noticed, had been very reserved the last few weeks. This worried him because she was his youngest child. He prayed for her future, not knowing what it would hold. He'd secretly hoped the older Montgomery boy would ask after her, but he hadn't. He'd found Emma Jenkins more appealing.

"Just as well," he said to himself. "She wouldn't be happy with anyone but Dewy anyhow."

A deep, rugged voice interrupted his thoughts. "Good afternoon, Mr. Townsend," said a stranger as he sat atop his horse, looking like he'd happened to be passing by, and yet he knew his name. "How are you fairing?"

"No complaints, sir, no complaints. Say, How might we be acquainted?" He asked as politely as possible, curious as to the answer.

"My apologies, sir. I should have made myself known." But he didn't need to say more. As soon as he smiled, Abel knew it was Dewy Montgomery.

"Come here, Lad." Dewy dismounted and they embraced for a long moment; all worries from before suddenly gone. As they released, he said in a broken tone: "Let me fetch Ellisa. I can't say how she'll respond to seeing you again, but I think it right good of you to come by on your way home." Dewy smiled with a new hope in his heart. If her father received him well, she might do the same. "Come in. Come in. Have a seat while I get her."

Ellisa's mother, Sarah, came out to view the visitor. She instantly knew who was seated in her living room. "Aren't you a sight for sore eyes?" Tears brimmed her face as she took in the man standing before her.

"Thank you. I apologize for my pungency. I've been traveling a long while."

"Nonsense." She waved his comment off. "We're so happy you've returned, regardless. Would you like a glass of tea while you wait?"

"Yes, Ma'am." Dewy agreed emphatically.

He heard Abel tell Ellisa she had a visitor, but didn't say who had come. He heard her sigh with annoyance and stop whatever she was doing to entertain someone. He heard her footsteps grow closer, but barely over the sound of his pounding heart.

He was finally here about to see his love for the first time in three years. The thought of running for the door scampered across his mind, but was brought to a sudden halt when she stood in the frame of the parlor door, staring at him, tears spilling down her face as recognition took hold of her understanding. Moments passed before she could move.

At last, she spoke. "Are you real? Is it you, or am I dreaming again? I don't think I would've dreamt a beard, but I like the look of it." A small grin graced her features before she stepped slowly towards him.

Dewy's breath hitched in his throat. He was unable to answer for a long moment. She was even more beautiful than he remembered, and had grown into a woman since the last day he'd laid eyes on her.

Tears freely coursed down his face as she stood in front of him. Dewy gulped before reaching one very timid hand out for her to take. "I've missed you so." He whispered. His voice had taken leave of his throat. She took his hand, and didn't resist as he kissed it.

"Dewy, I've missed you more than I can express. I cannot say how elated I am that you've come back to me. I'm sorry I was angry with you. I never stopped loving you." Sobs took over her slight figure again.

Dewy shook his head, placing one finger on her mouth. "It is I who must apologize to you. I will never leave you again, if you'll still have me."

"Mr. Townsend?" Dewy coughed out, unable to tear his eyes away from Ellisa's.

"Yes, Dewy?" Mr. Townsend came into view. He obviously hadn't been too far away.

Dewy pulled Ellisa to his chest, stroking her hair, smelling her familiar sweet scent. "May I marry your daughter? I mean, I know I've asked once already, but I feel I should make a second inquiry, considering." He pulled her back enough to look into her eyes. "I hope she still wants me. I've thought of nothing but Ellisa for the last three years. I can't imagine spending another day without her."

"If she wants you, I have no objection. Make her happy or you answer to me." Abel said, attempting a stern voice, but failing for his own joy at the return of his daughter's true love.

Dewy looked into Ellisa's eyes, though he was still speaking with her father. "I love her. I won't ever leave her again as long as I live." Directing his speech to her again, Dewy continued. "I will fight for you, for us. I'll die if it means keeping you safe. I'm not perfect, but..." Ellisa raised herself onto her toes and kissed Dewy fully and in front of her father.

A few seconds passed before Abel Townsend, though amused, cleared his throat to signal they'd taken that embrace far enough.

Dewy's voice was low and gruff, causing a delightful shiver to run up Ellisa's spine. "Elle ... I have to go. I have to make things right with my father." She nodded, but kissed Dewy one more time before he shook Abel's hand and hugged Sarah again. "I'll see you very soon. I love you. Thank you for believing in me."

He walked out, untied Bess, saddled up and rode towards home as quickly as possible.

A Seat at the Table

He could smell the goose and sweet potatoes cooking in the kitchen. His mother never failed to amaze him with the food she prepared. "Hello, Ma! That is some delicious smell coming from your kitchen." He winked, hugging her.

"What news, Philip?" Tilly asked as her son kissed her cheek, handed her a bouquet of flowers and a bottle of wine for dinner.

"Not much. The train came as I was leaving town, but I didn't wait to see who needed a ride. Most people are preparing for Thanksgiving. I'm asking after Emma Jenkins." He smiled as his mother gushed her approval.

"You sly dog; isn't she in mourning?" His sister, also named Emma, asked as she put the flowers into a vase.

"Yes, but she says mourning is for the old people and we have to live our lives. She also said pining after Joseph won't bring him back." Philip's smile told on his emotions.

"She's a smart girl." Mary agreed while taking the wine bottle to the kitchen to chill on a block of ice Pa had brought up from the cellar.

"That she is, and beautiful, too." Philip had never before blushed in his life until that moment.

"I'd say he's besotted, girls, by the looks of him." Gaius laughed as he came inside the kitchen door and hugged his son. Philip expected some ribbing from his family, and wasn't embarrassed in the least. He was certainly smitten.

"Leave him alone, the lot of you. Dinner will be ready shortly. Mary, Emma, could you ask the older children to help set?" Tilly smiled, handing them each plates for the dinner table.

"I'm going outside for a few moments, Ma. I'll tell them." Philip volunteered as he smiled, grabbed his pipe out of his jacket, and ambled to the front door, whistling a lively tune that reminded him of Emma Jenkins. Maybe someday, soon he hoped she'd be Emma Montgomery.

"Nana Montgomery needs your help setting the table," he jovially announced to the children. "I'll stay and watch the others so you can help." The children dashed to the porch. "Don't forget to clean your shoes, or she'll hand you the mop bucket after dinner." He joked and patted them on the back as they did as he'd instructed.

He struck the match to stoke his pipe, wishing he'd brought along his banjo. That would certainly keep them entertained for the next few minutes until his mother was ready for them to sit down. He drew a long breath on his pipe, thinking of a raven-haired girl and her deep green eyes. He looked around the yard, and remembrances seemed to circle him like ghosts from the past.

A bonfire raged; teen girls giggling and boys laughing, lively music playing, Dewy flirting with Ellisa Townsend between songs. Ma walked outside often enough to make sure no one was acting unseemly. Many times, Clem brought his violin for accompaniment and Joseph Carmichael played Ma's washboard with a spoon for a form of percussion. Good times.

Philip looked up, seeing a ghost on a horse coming straight up the road. He knew then that the past was coming to life.

Until the ghost waved at him, dismounted and walked towards him.

He wasn't an exact replica of his brother, but an older, wiser, more mature looking version of his little bratty sibling.

Then, the apparition called out to him.

"Philip! God, it's good to see you! You look dashing as ever!" It was certainly Dewy's voice, but no longer acted like or resembled him. For a moment, Philip didn't move, breathe, or acknowledge him; too stunned to act.

"Don't stand there like a statue. Come here and let me shake your hand."

"No!" Philip's one syllable reply caused Dewy to draw back like he'd shot a gun instead of greeting him.

"What? What do you mean by 'no'?" Dewy reeled from his brother's response. After the reception in town, he figured everyone would be equally excited to welcome him home. His mother's last letter even said that much.

"I mean, after all this time with no word..."

"I sent word. I've written to Ma from the start; Ellisa too!"

"Not once to me, Brother. As far as I'm concerned, you died in that War, leaving me to everything here in regards to the family. You best get on your horse and go. No one here wants to see you."

"Come, now, Philip. I do apologize for not writing you, but you don't speak for Ma and Paw when you say those things." Dewy's voice remained calm, but inside, his heart was breaking. How could he be so calloused?

A little too loudly, Philip made his position clear. "I said, you best be getting on down the road, boy. There's no one here who wants to see you! You've broken too many hearts, and left too much pain in your wake to come back like the past three years haven't happened! LEAVE!"

The front door slammed against the external wall of the house and Gaius's voice thundered as he stepped out. "What the devil's going on?" He viewed the scene before him. "Philip?"

Philip turned and quickly met his father in the yard. "It's nothing, Paw; just some vagabond who wants to come and eat up our food. Probably wants to rob you!" Philip's words made Dewy wish he could sink into a hole in the ground. They weren't true, but obviously Philip felt like they could be. Dewy had no idea the pain went so deep with his brother.

"I'll be the judge of that. Go on in and tell your Ma everything's fine here. I'll be inside momentarily." He eyed his son, hoping he'd calm down once indoors. He focused on the man who stood a ways off, and obviously Philip had walked out a distance to see him. He looked at him for a long moment before asking how he could help the lost man.

"Now, what can I ..?" Recognition lit Gaius's eyes as he realized who was standing there. "Andrew? Is it? My, you've grown up on me, son."

His heart burst with joy! Gaius began walking to meet Dewy, but the distance couldn't close fast enough. He felt the wind at his face as his pace increased, until he was trotting a bit to get a closer look at his son. Soon, he was sprinting, as if running towards a burning house to save the trapped inhabitants. His feet were not swift enough for him. He longed to hold his son in his arms, to make right all the wrongs he'd dealt the boy all those years ago.

As Dewy watched him approach, he was scared like a little child about to get a lesson behind the wood shed. His knees shook and his breathing went shallow while his heart pounded through his chest like a thousand stampeding horses. As his father reached him, he fell to his knees, sobbing like a babe.

Guilt hammered him to the ground, and from his soul, he poured out his agony. "I'm so sorry, Pa. So sorry! I never should've left. I never should've gone against your wishes. The things I've seen, done, I ... I don't deserve to come home, but please, let me work the land as a farm hand for you. Please, won't you forgive me?"

Large, patient hands scooped under his arms and pulled him to his feet and into a warm embrace. "That's foolishness, Andrew; utter foolishness." He whispered to his grown boy. "Look at me, Son." Dewy drew back and looked his father in the eye for the first time in three years. Tears streamed from the elder man's sky blue eyes, wetting his beard, and a smile formed on his face. "You are my son! I need your forgiveness." His voice wavered, but his strength did not. "I raised you to do what was right, and you felt it was right to go fight for freedom. I never should've forbidden it, and I was wrong to be angry with you." The two estranged men embraced for a long moment. "Now that we have that out in the open, I know a woman who would love to wrap her arms around her baby boy! Your mother is a prayin' woman."

"I know it, Pa. I believe her prayers kept me alive. There's so much to tell. But, this I will tell you now: Ellisa and I are going to marry, soon I hope." He was radiant with joy at his father's welcome.

"That certainly is grand news. We better get your house built. You're going to want a place all your own." He laughed, slapped Dewy on the back and grinned all the more. "Come on, son. There's a seat at the table just for you."

~~~~~

From the front door, Gaius called out: "Tilly, come here for a moment, love."

He heard her exhale loudly, put down whatever pan she'd been holding, and walk towards the parlor. She sucked in a deep breath when she saw the man standing there with her husband, and before words could come out, she sobbed loudly.

Dewy let the tears flow unimpeded as he opened his arms and surrounded his mother in a long-overdue embrace. For a long moment, they stood there without saying anything.

"Oh, God, at last," she breathed out "my son has come back to me. Let me look at you boy." Tilly stroked his beard, chuckling through her tears. "No! You're not a boy any longer, are you? Come, let's eat. The table is set and I'm sure you're hungry."

"Yes, Ma, I certainly am." Dewy chuckled as relief flooded his being.

As they entered the dining room, both Mary and Dewy's twin sister, Emma, jumped up and ran to him, embracing him; Mary a little longer, and with a few more tears because of her loss. The children cheered and rallied around him. William, Emma's husband, stood patiently waiting in the background for a chance to say hello.

Philip stood, scraping the chair loudly against the floor, and stomped out through the kitchen door to the barn yard. Gaius, not missing anything, patted Tilly's shoulder and walked through to talk to his son.

Philip's voice was a little too loud and his pain all too evident. "Pa. How could you? How could you possibly allow him back after all this time? He caused Ma to cry for years, your smile to leave, and you welcome him like some hero?" HIs voiced edged up a pitch with every question; the hurt evident in his voice. "I've been here the whole time, always checking to make sure you and Ma were doing well, and seeing to my sisters. And this is how I am repaid? By spitting in my face and acting like Dewy is the long lost Prodigal?"

Gaius let him finish his tirade before answering in his ever-even-tone. "Yes, Philip. Just like the story from the Good Book. He was lost and is found. He was dead. Or he could've been dead.

He's home. Don't you see? Mary's Joe didn't come home, nor did Emma Jenkins' love. We have a rare gift staring us in the face: Our soldier, my son, your brother, is here on Thanksgiving Day. We have much for which to be thankful!" He touched his son on the shoulder gently. "Pray a moment, and then come sit at table with us and enjoy the blessing our Lord has literally dropped at our doorstep: Andrew! Home! Alive! "

~~~~~

As they bowed their heads to pray, Philip walked into the dining room. He stood in the door moment before heaving a deep breath. Dewy stood, walked to his brother, and held his hand out for Philip to shake. "Forgive me, brother. I had no idea how wounded you all were from my absence. I shall make it up to you, somehow."

"I forgive you, Dewy. Forgive me for not welcoming you. I love you and I thank the Good Lord that you live." They embraced, both brothers fighting the torrent of emotions that ruled the day.

Gaius broke in: "Good! Now that all's forgiven, we can eat. Andrew, will you ask the blessing?"

"Yessir." He responded and began as everyone bowed for the prayer. "Thank you, Lord." He paused, reining in his emotions again. "Thank you for getting me home." A torrent of tears threatened every eye at the table. "Thank you for forgiveness and love. Thank you for the many blessings we're privileged to have. We thank you for the gift of family. Most importantly, we thank you for the gift of love you gave us when you saved us. We ask you to bless this food. In your holy, righteous name we pray, Amen." Everyone echoed the Amen and began passing food one to another.

Dewy sighed as he heaped food on his plate. It was the most he'd had in a while, and best of all, it was his mother's cooking.

He could not have imagined this homecoming any better if he tried. He was reconciled to his family, his love, and, most importantly, his Lord. His journey surely had been long, but now that it was over, he could begin a new journey. The Prodigal Son was finally home.

The Future Awaits

Journal of Andrew Dwight "Dewy" Montgomery

December 1, 1865

The past few days had been most wonderful with the family. Ma made up my bed for me in my room, and before dawn the next morning, Pa had me up milking cows and collecting eggs. We worked the fallow ground closest to the house and harvested the garden so Ma could put up stores for winter. Not that it gets terribly cold here, but we'll have plenty of time without much to do.

Philip, though a bit distant still, is coming around. He sat on the porch on Thanksgiving night with Pa and I, smoking pipes and talking about irrelevant things. He seems to be quite taken with Clem's little sister, and for that, I am glad. They will be very happy together.

This afternoon, Pa and I went to search out a plot of land for my home. We'll start building in March if the weather's good. We don't expect snow, but one never knows with the weather in Texas. Some years past, we had so much rain that we had to plant later than we wanted. I must say, I am very excited to show Ellisa where we'll be building. It's a bit closer to town, but still on Montgomery land. It's all planned out in my mind, but I want her to have an opinion.

Life in Comfort goes on. The town continues to grow, and those lost are not forgotten. I feel a bit left behind, as life continued while I was away at war. So much has changed.

Sunday after service, we're having a good old fashioned get together. Pa said he'll build a fire, and most of the town is invited to come. Not so much to recreate the good times we had, but perhaps we'll make new memories; memories to last a lifetime.

~~~~~

"Andrew! Andrew, wake up now, son. We've chores to tend to." Gaius knocked on the door of his son's room. He felt, with Dewy's presence, a liberation from the burden he'd carried for those years of his son's absence. Really, he felt it as soon as he set eyes on the boy.

The biggest change he'd seen was in Philip. He was coming over every day at noon and staying until late into the evening. How he ever accomplished any work was beyond Gaius, but he'd leave that to Philip. He was his own man.

"I'm up, Pa. I'll be out in a moment." Gaius heard Dewy from the other side of the door. Tilly walked out of their room at that moment, drawing her hand slowly across his lower back as she passed to go to the kitchen. Gaius caught her hand, kissed it, and pulled her back toward their bedroom.

"Dewy, I'll be down in a bit."

"This early dear? Dewy's home ... and ..." Tilly blushed, thinking of her husband's intentions.

"And he's a grown man. He can handle the chores. I have other..." a small laugh escaped, "things to tend to this day."

"What about breakfast?" Tilly argued, even as her husband shut the bedroom door.

"He'll be alright, love. Come back to bed for a bit." Gaius cooed quietly; the sound of his voice both soothing and sending pleasant shivers through her body.

"You're incorrigible."

"That I am, but you like me this way." Gaius whispered as he rained kisses on his wife.

"I do. I love you exactly like you are: Stubborn, stuck in your ways, and very good as kissing." Tilly smiled and Gaius picked her up like she was his new bride, carrying her to their bed.

"Good, because I don't plan on changing this late in life." His whispers continued.

~~~~~

The day had gone on in a very typical way. Ma and Pa were a bit late getting up, but Dewy managed pretty well to get the morning chores finished, make his own breakfast, and go for a stroll to revisit his building site. At the moment, he was moving hay for the animals, trying to stay busy and be useful.

A wagon coming up the dirt drive caught Dewy's attention. He loved that about his parents' property. The road only led to their home. A person had to purpose to visit them. People didn't just pass by, though Dewy was glad for all those who had homes at the roadsides when he was on his journey.

Today, he planned on going further out on the farm, riding Bess and getting a feel for being a farmer again. For three long years, being a soldier had been his life, and he had loved it. He missed it sometimes. Maybe, he thought to himself, he would take his rifle with him and hunt while he was out. They could process and store the meat for winter. Sometimes a man just needed to smell gunpowder.

A hand waved from the wagon before he could decide who was visiting. Putting down his pitch fork, Dewy dusted his hands on his pants and went towards the front. A smile broke out across his bearded face as he realized who was visiting.

"Mr. and Mrs. Townsend, Ellisa? What brings you visiting this fine day?" Dewy asked as they brought the wagon to a stop. Dewy reached up to aid Ellisa down from the seat as her father aided her mother. He looked deeply into her eyes, kissing her hand simultaneously.

"Your mother invited us for tea and then dinner tonight." Ellisa said quietly, a bit of uncertainty lacing her tone. "I hope you agree with the decision."

"Of course I do, but I would've cleaned up first had I known you were coming today." He apologetically looked down at his dirty clothes and hands before giving her a wry grin.

"I'm only happy I get to see you, dirty or clean." Ellisa's smile sent Dewy's heart soaring.

"Let's go inside and I'll tell Ma you're here." He took her hand as they slowly walked toward the house. Opening the front door, Dewy saw no sign of his mother. His father was also nowhere to be seen. He called out, but didn't hear an answer.

"Well, I'll search them out. Please make yourselves at home." Dewy asked, politely but with a bit of worry in his voice.

He went towards their room, but the door was open and neither was there. He looked in the kitchen, the great room, and finally in the root cellar. His parents were not there. When he came up from the cellar, his mother's voice echoed from the barn. He didn't understand anything she said, but she sounded happy enough.

He shook his head and went to the well to draw a bit of water. His parents seemed more contented with one another than ever. Just before he headed inside with the water, he simply called out: "Ma, Pa. We have company. The Townsends are here. Do hurry on with your, uh, chores, won't you?" He could no longer stifle a laugh as he heard his mother gasp and his father swear.

Loud whispers followed before his mother, with a few wayward pieces of straw in her hair and all over her dress, walked out of the barn with pink in her cheeks and a grin on her face. Gaius followed looking like a rooster after a hen.

"Uh, thank you, son, for announcing their arrival. Do tell them we'll be right in, would you?" Tilly asked, all grace under her son's scrutiny.

"Yes ma'am." Dewy smiled, shook his head, and walked inside. He washed his hands and face, set water on to boil for tea, and found a dessert his mother had made the night before to take to the Townsends.

"They will be in shortly." Dewy simply announced, trying with all his might to neither laugh nor give away his parents' secret rendezvous in the barn.

~~~~~

Tea, dinner, and dessert passed in a blur of storytelling from everyone, laughter, and even a little dancing in the parlor. Dewy could not stop watching Ellisa; her movements, her unassuming yet elegant nature, her sweet spirit. He wanted so much to steal her away for a while, but every time he thought he might, someone would ask a question or make a suggestion. All in all, he was beyond elated just to be with her, her family, and his parents. This, Dewy thought, was why he'd gone to war.

"Penny for your thoughts, Son?" Gaius asked as he stepped out and lit his pipe on the front step while Dewy gazed absent-mindedly at the sky, watching the colors of the sunset.

"Nothing really worth sharing. This has been an absolutely wonderful day, and I am overwhelmed with joy at the moment. But, before the sun is gone completely, I want to take Ellisa out to our land. Our land. Those words don't seem real. You know, I haven't even asked her to marry me? Not in those exact words. I asked her father; received his blessing, but since I've returned, I have yet to propose properly."

"I think you know what you need to do. I'd wager, if I were a gambling man, it's what you want to do as well." Dewy nodded at his father's exhortation. "But, before you do, I want to say one more piece." Dewy seemed to straighten, almost as if he were waiting for his father to give advice, or correct him somehow. Gaius reached out, resting his hand on his youngest son's shoulder.

"What is it, Pa?" Dewy asked quietly.

"We cannot take back those years of anger and regret. We can only move forward. I-" his voice cracked slightly, causing Dewy to lose what little hold he had on his emotions. "I'm proud of you, son. I'm proud of the man you've become while you were away. Now, go get that beautiful girl and do what needs doing!"

"Yes sir." Dewy answered, wiping a tear from his eye before hugging his father for a long moment. "Thank you."

~~~~~

With permission from her parents given, Dewy hitched Bess up to his carriage and aimed south towards town.

"Where are we going, Dewy?" Ellisa asked as she placed her hand in his elbow.

"It's a surprise." He smiled, kissed her cheek, and clucked his tongue to get Bess to pick up her pace. They rode in a companionable silence for ten minutes before he pulled the reins, slowing the wagon to a stop.

Ellisa looked around at the wood placed on the ground. Some of it was laid out as if someone were in the beginning stages of building something. The rest of it was stacked neatly a few yards away. Other things were about, like saw horses, tools, and shovels.

"What is this?" She asked quietly.

"I think facing North to South is a good plan, that way the sunlight comes in all day: Sun from the East in the morning, and the orange glow from the West in the evening. And it should have a wraparound porch, a root cellar just over there, and at least four bedrooms: One downstairs for visitors, and the others on the second floor. I think an indoor bath would be good, too. What do you think?" Dewy asked with a far-away look in his eyes, as though he were speaking to someone about building his house.

"What are you talking about, Dewy? It all seems grand, but I have no idea what is going on in that head of yours." Ellisa shook her head, trying to understand him.

"It's the house, Elle. Where should I put the kitchen? Should we build a parlor and a great room, or keep it small? I mean, hopefully it will be full sooner than later, but at first ..." Dewy stared at the road as he spoke.

"Andrew Dwight Montgomery, for crying out loud, what are you talking about?" Her voice came out distressed, bringing his attention to her concerned features.

"I'm sorry." He took her hand, kissed it, and knelt down, not on one knee, but two. "I should have done this as soon as I saw you again, Elle. My sweet, sincere Elle."

Her breath stopped in her throat. "Dewy?"

"Ellisa Townsend, in a previous life, you said yes, but now, here on what I hope will one day soon be our home, I want to ask again." He kissed her hands slowly. "Will you be my wife? Will you have this wretched man? I know I hurt you when I left, but with God, and ole Bess over there, as my witnesses, I'll never leave you again. I will be a good husband to you. I'll work hard all day, and every night, I'll love you like you deserve to be loved." Ellisa blushed at his inuendos about married life. "What do you say, Elle? Will you?"

"Oh, do shut up and kiss me, Dewy." She squealed as he pulled her down to the ground, somehow landing her on his lap.

"Yes ma'am."

After several intense kisses, Ellisa pulled away from Dewy, bracing his face with her gloved hands.

"Yes. I still want you. I never stopped hoping or praying that you'd come back. I never stopped loving you, even when I was angry and injured at heart over your departure. I knew that if you died..." She paused, closing her eyes and leaning so that her forehead rested on his, sniffing back the tears before they escaped. "I knew I'd never marry anyone but you, Dewy. You're the only man I want, have ever wanted, or ever will want. I want to be your wife, the mother of your children, your constant companion and lover for all my years." She did not give Dewy a chance to speak again for several long moments more.

"How soon is enough time to get this wedding ready?" He asked in a low, husky voice. She shivered a little with delight as he wrapped his arms around her to pull her close.

"I shall ask mother and father tonight on our way home. The sooner, the better for me. I don't even mind if we live in your parents' home, or mine, or even alternate between them until the house is finished." She breathed.

After a few more shared embraces, they rode back to the house, talking all the way about the house, children, what crops to plant, and every other plan they could make until they reached the barnyard. Dewy quickly put Bess up and walked back out front.

As they were approaching the door, Ellisa stopped him once more. "Kiss me one more time before we go inside."

"I look forward to kissing you good and often." He laughed before bending to oblige her once more.

"And I look forward to being kissed good and often, my love." She giggled a delightfully. "Now, let's go tell our family the happy news." They joined hands and walked inside.

Hope filled their future and all was right with the world.

Epilogue - Blessings Abound

T he Montgomery Ranch

Christmas Day

1865

"You are positively glowing, Ellisa." Emma hugged her best friend from childhood with a large grin gracing her own features.

"As are you my dear friend. How's married life treating you?" Ellisa squeezed Emma Jenkins-Montgomery's hand in a thoughtful gesture. She and Philip had married the first week in December. It was difficult at first, not being so close to one another, but they found that the family gatherings were a great place to catch up.

"It's positively wonderful." Emma's response was accompanied by a sigh of satisfaction. "I couldn't ask for a better husband, and he's still very attentive. He comes home every day for the noon meal, and then stays far longer than he should." She giggled, and Ellisa joined her. "So, how do you like married life?"

"I … no words can describe how right it feels to be by Dewy's side. I'd say we both did very well in marrying the Montgomery boys. And now, we really are sisters. Though, I dare say, I am anxious to be in my own home. I mean, I did tell Dewy it was alright if we lived with relatives until it was built, but it has been a long month and a half."

"Well, the two of you didn't exactly leave any proper planning time for a wedding. If you had waited until spring, you might've had a home ready for you."

"It's true. I was ready to be married to Dewy as soon as he showed up in my parents' parlor. Preacher Harvey was all too kind to marry us as quickly as he did. He said, and I quote: 'Love has no timeline or limit. If you know this is what the Good Lord wants for you, then I'm glad to marry you.' Two weeks later, well, you know the rest of the story."

"Oh yes, as does the rest of Comfort, Texas. It didn't give us too much time to ready anything, but I can't complain. I'm really so happy for you both." Emma patted her knee, sitting down next to Ellisa, who was knitting. "What are you knitting?"

"Oh, this is just another gift for Dewy. He's been out back with Gaius and William, as is Jacob Rathburn."

"Jacob Rathburn. He's rather new in town? Interesting that he's invited here for Christmas dinner, isn't it?" Emma said quizzically.

"Well, it seems Mary has captured his eye. I think it's wonderful. After Joe died, she was a shell of a woman. Now, she's smiling and laughing again. He also happens to have a son, and he seems to adore her children. Sometimes the Lord does strange things. I think this happens to be wonderful for her. She deserves a good man. Who knows? There might be another wedding happening sooner than we think." Ellisa was equally glad they were off the subject of her knitting project.

"That would be fantastic. I'm going to wander into the kitchen to see if Tilly needs, or wants, any more help." Emma smiled as she stood.

"I'll be there as soon as I finish this last row."

Emma, though she didn't voice her thoughts, knew exactly what Ellisa was knitting. She could barely contain her joy for her best friend.

~~~~~

Philip joined the other men out in the barnyard as they helped Gaius butcher the deer he'd killed the day before. The roast had to be drained completely and then someone would run it to the kitchen so that Tilly could put it on for Christmas dinner.

"Hi there, little brother. How are you handling having a wife around?" He goaded Dewy as he shook his hand.

"To quote the Good Book: 'He who finds a wife finds a good thing.'" Dewy said with mirth in his voice. "I have a very good thing."

"Yes, you do, son," Gaius chimed in as he and William continued skinning the deer, "but you need to take your good thing to your own home soon. The way those two keep company, they'll have a brood of children much quicker than they anticipate." Everyone laughed at his expense, but Dewy stood grinning like a boy in a candy store.

"A very good thing!" Dewy repeated. "I suspect she's already in the family way, though she's not said anything to me about it yet. She seems to sleep quite a bit, and doesn't feel so well when she awakens."

"A woman takes great pride in telling her husband she's having his child, so wait for her announcement. But, from the sounds of it, I'd say you are most likely correct." Gaius looked up at his son, smiling. "And if you grin any wider, your face might split in half!" The other men were once again laughing.

"Jacob." Dewy turned the conversation's attention away from himself. "How are things with Mary?"

"They are very good. I, uh, have to talk to Gaius before I can say any more than that." At Jacob's admission, Gaius stopped, put down his knife, and turned to look at the man.

"You don't need my permission. She's no longer mine to give. She was married once, and you know what she's gone through these past few months. But, if it's my blessing you want, you have it. Take care of my daughter and grandchildren. They have some happiness coming their way." Gaius picked up his knife and went back to his work.

"Thank you, Mr..."

"It's Gaius. We're all family here."

Jacob grinned, patting the breast pocket of his coat. "Then, I may do the asking after Christmas dinner."

"We're happy to have you in the family, Jacob." Dewy was the first to say, shaking Jacob's hand. Philip was next.

William looked on, smiling. "I'm equally happy for you, but won't shake your hand until we're done here." He motioned to the almost-finished deer.

Gaius said nothing more, but the tears threatened his features, and he had to breathe deeply to maintain his composure.

Tilly's voice chimed out: "Is that roast almost ready? We won't eat until midnight if it takes too much longer." Gaius grinned to himself as she approached them. He and Tilly were enjoying this: The whole family, with all the new additions and the laughter going on around them.

"Yes. We'll have it to you momentarily." Gaius answered as she came up to his side.

"Here's the dish for it. Thank you for all the hard work, my love." She leaned in to him so no one else heard what she was saying, and whispered a few words meant only for his ears. Gaius's grin broadened and a sparkle lit his blue eyes. Tilly kissed him, knowing full well he couldn't reciprocate because his hands were messy, and went back inside.

The other four men gathered there didn't seem to, or tried not to, notice the exchange. They chatted on about hunting, crops, and other things until the deer meat had been hung to dry and the skin was ready for tanning.

Gaius thanked the Lord for all the blessings of the past two months as he went to wash up before going inside. The laughter of the children seemed to echo all over outside, causing the aging man to continue smiling. He was certainly grateful for all the Lord had brought them and especially for his growing family.

~~~~~

After the family had eaten, they gathered in the parlor for gifts and carols. Philip and Dewy even took out their instruments.

"We'll build a bonfire out front after dark. But, first, let's get this gift giving started." Gaius announced. "Philip: Would you and Emma start?" And so it went. They gave and received gifts for over an hour.

Dewy and Philip had built an extension for the dining room table to accommodate all of the family members, as well as six more chairs. They even joked about building onto the actual dining room as the one Tilly and Gaius now inhabited seems to be shrinking.

Mary cried when Jacob knelt down and proposed in front of the whole family. He even asked the children's permission to marry their Maw. They responded by jumping on him and knocking him to the floor, chanting "Yes" over and over.

Gaius and Tilly gave each of their children, and families, a set of china as well as a quilt that Tilly had been working on overtime for several months. Apparently, she'd had secret quilting bees to help finish them all in time for the holiday celebration.

William and Emma announced a new addition would be joining the family around August. When Tilly started crying, the men all laughed and the women all began crying.

Dewy also built a beautiful headboard, matching Chester drawers and night tables for Ellisa. "For our new house." She cried.

Ellisa finally had her turn to give Dewy his gifts. The first was a pocket watch she'd been given from her father. The second was a new shirt she'd made herself. She handed him the smallest, saying, "Last one, I promise."

Dewy looked at her oddly. "What's this?" He asked, opening the minutely wrapped package. Inside, he gazed for a moment before looking at her with wonder and more love than he'd ever held for her. "Is this what I think it is?" His voice caught on unshed emotions. She nodded, wordlessly. Dewy gazed into her beautiful face, watched her gulp as the tears began spilling from her eyes.

"Well, what is it?" An impatient child asked from somewhere in the room. At that moment, Dewy only felt Ellisa's presence. The rest of the family could have disappeared for all he knew.

"It's a pair of baby booties and a cap. Really?" Ellisa once again nodded at his question before he stood and scooped her up in his arms, spinning her around while they both simultaneously laughed and cried.

Cheers went up around the parlor and they began singing a Christmas Carol.

~~~~~

May 1866

Ellisa let out a ragged breath while sitting down on her mother-in-laws settee in the parlor of their home. She and Dewy had spent the first six months of their married life in his parents' home, visiting with her parents from time to time to give the Montgomery's a well-deserved break from having family around the house and underfoot constantly.

She circled her swelling abdomen with her palm all the while still attempting to catch her breath. No matter what Tilly said, Ellisa refused to sit idly by while the older woman did the majority of the housework.

At present, Tilly was making lemonade. Ellisa had just taken the bread for dinner from the oven before sitting down. The cookies she'd baked that morning were sitting in a covered plate, and the thought of eating one, or several, appealed to her state of being at the moment.

Tilly, smiling, walked in with a tray.

"You read my mind. I was thinking those cookies would be perfect for a snack about now." Ellisa chuckled, offering to pour the lemonade.

"I remember when I was expecting. I baked like a mad woman, and loved sampling the goods afterwards. Yes, every single Montgomery for three generations has been born here. Do you think Dewy will have the house finished before the baby comes?" At Tilly's question, Ellisa's face twisted and tears began to fall unexpectedly. "Oh, my. I've said something to hurt you, dear. I didn't mean anything by it! I was thinking how nice it would be for a fourth generation." Ellisa's tears came all the harder.

"It seems he'll never get that house finished, and I might just be with child forever." Ellisa cried until she began laughing. "Does it always feel this hopeless?"

"Only the last few months, I promise. All will be well. This part, especially with the weather as warm as it is, can be difficult on a woman in your condition. I'm sure Dewy and Gaius and all the others are trying their best to finish so you can have your own home. I know Dewy is anxious to get moved. Gaius and I love you both very much, and it's been wonderful having you stay with us."

Before Ellisa could respond, Dewy ran into the parlor. "Come on. I have something to show you." The women looked puzzled, but went outside, where Dewy had Bess hitched to the wagon.

"I don't think I can get up into the wagon, dear." Dewy had already thought of a solution, and moved a box to help her climb into the bed. "What is this? Dewy? What's going on?"

He smiled, helped his mother into the wagon seat, and signaled the horse to go with a "hyauh." The horse began walking at a fast clip, making the wagon lurch into motion. These were not comfortable days, Ellisa thought to herself. They were moving towards town. She worried she wasn't ready for town, and it would be a long ride without a bonnet or parasol to keep the sun off her face.

Dewy stopped the wagon, hopped down, and walked to the back to Ellisa. "How are you both today?" He asked gently, placing a hand on her round belly. He had been gone since before the sun was up. "Sorry for all the bumps." He leaned in, kissing her intently, before asking, "Would you mind very much closing your eyes for the remainder of the journey? It won't be much longer, but I have a surprise for you and I want to see your face when you open your eyes."

Ellisa giggled before responding with: "All right. They're closed." She let out an "oof" when the wagon started moving again. An eternity passed before she felt it coming to a halt once more.

"I'm going to help you get down, love, but do be careful." Dewy announced as Ellisa felt the brake engage on the wheel, and the load lighten as the front two passengers were unloaded.

"I don't think I could get down alone at this stage, dear." She felt his weight in the bed as he hopped up. He lifted her gently by the arm, helping her stand.

"Alright now. Easy does it. Here's the edge. I'm going to hop down, and then help you." He moved something that scraped the wagon, and then eased her foot down until she felt the wooden box he'd used at the house. "Keep those pretty eyes closed, love. We're almost there."

They walked for a moment, Dewy watching her every footstep to make sure she didn't fall. He turned her around, and Ellisa heard Tilly gasp. "Open your eyes, love." Dewy said in a whisper.

"It's a field, Dewy." Ellisa said, all of the excitement of the moment gone.

"I know." He grinned impishly. "Turn around." He laughed and kissed her right behind the ear, sending a delightful feeling through her being.

Before her was the most beautiful sight she'd ever seen: Their house.

Tears pricked at the corner of her eyes, and her lower lip began to tremble. Dewy, too busy grinning to notice, turned to see his bride's face twisting.

"Elle, what is it? Why are you crying?" Dewy took her shoulders in a soft grip to force her to look at him.

"It's... it's ... so ... b-b-b-beautiful. Our house! Dewy! You've done wonderfully! I love it! I'm just so h-h-ha-happ…" She placed a hand over her mouth as her face became wet with tears for a second time in not so many hours.

Dewy surrounded her with his arms, kissing her hair, and biting his lip to withhold his laughter. His mother and father stood a ways off, in a similar embrace, grinning broadly and seemingly attempting to keep their merriment at bay.

Dewy remembered complaining to Gaius only a c ouple of weeks ago about her moods; how one moment she was happy and the next she could be spitting nails, or bawling like a babe. Gaius laughed and said, "It goes with the child she carries. Your ma was near impossible to live with when she was in a family way. But, if you love her, you'll find that it will all be worthwhile in the end."

This, Dewy surmised, was one moment he would chalk up to childbearing. He felt her relax a bit, and he looked into her beautiful face. "Come see the rest. I think you'll be pleased. It's planned out exactly, and there's so much to see."

He remembered his surprise for her in the nursery, and made sure he had his handkerchief ready. She'd cry again.

"Here's the porch. It wraps all the way around, so we can enjoy the seasons and any time of day. We also have a door that opens from our bedroom. Pa, Philip and I worked on these chairs and benches for three days. We'll be able to host a grand gathering once you're up to it. Come on, lemme show you the kitchen."

Dewy gently lifted her up and carried her over the threshold and into the house. Ellisa giggled, forgetting her sobbing from a moment ago. The front room, or parlor, had a grand fireplace, bookshelves on both sides and a few pieces of furniture throughout; including a settee and couch.

"Where's this furniture come from? Dewy, we cannot possibly aff..."

"Your parents, that's where. Let me worry about what we can and cannot afford. We're going to be fine. Come on, there's much more to see." He tugged her hand gently as he led her to the right and into the dining room. There were four chairs and an oak table.

"We'll add more chairs as we need them." He kissed her cheek as he led her into her new kitchen. He had made cabinets and countertops that went half way around the room, a small table in the center with two chairs and a high chair. Ellisa smiled up at him, her eyes glistening once again. He opened one cabinet and showed her the china they'd been given at Christmas, as well as some other dishes. "Of course, you can rearrange these things in any way you want them. I brought all of our things over, secretively, so they'd be here when we finished." His grin made her heart skip a beat or two, and loved consumed her.

"That was so thoughtful of you. Thank you." He pulled her to a small hallway just outside the kitchen. "What's this?" He simply opened the first door to reveal an indoor washroom, complete with a closing stool that hid the waste under it and a wash basin. The porcelain claw-foot bathing tub took her breath away.

"I don't have to go outside in the dark anymore? That's wonderfully thoughtful of you! I imagine, you are going to benefit from it as well." She giggled.

"I also won't have to worry about your safety. And it will be part of my first thing chores every day. You won't have to worry about any unseemly smells. Come, there's more to see." They continued to the next door, and when it opened, Ellisa's face could not contain her smile. Their bedroom furniture that he'd given her for Christmas fit perfectly into the room with plenty of space to move about, as well. He'd added her Hope chest as well as a rocking chair and decorative lamps. There was a second door against the right wall, and when she opened it, it went into the washroom. Ellisa's heart leapt with joy.

"It's perfect, Dewy. The best room in the house." She said quietly for his parents' sake. The look she gave him was unmistakable. Dewy nodded, kissed her quickly, and proceeded out of the room to the next one across the hall. There she saw another bedroom, smaller but similar to their master.

"Nice room, dear. For guests?"

"For now. As the children grow, this will become theirs. We also built a loft over the great room which is empty for now, but will be a bedroom someday. There's one more bedroom to show you, and then we'll go out back and I'll show you the barn, the root cellar, and the well." They walked back towards the master bedroom and he opened another door, allowing her to go in first.

Ellisa was once again breathless. The cradle sat near the inside left wall, a small dresser sat opposite the cradle with a rail, and a rocker sat near the window. As predicted, the water started streaming from her eyes once again, causing Dewy to force back a chuckle before handing her his handkerchief and drawing her into his embrace.

"The house is absolutely everything I dreamed. When do we get to ..." she blushed at the thought of the question she was trying to ask.

"Tonight, love, if you would like. I know Ma and Paw are anxious to have their house to themselves again, even if they won't say so." He laughed, smoothed her hair, and kissed her. "But, if you want to wait a few more days..." Ellisa's finger over his lips hushed him quickly.

"NO! Tonight is perfect. If you have food ready, I can even cook in our new kitchen." She smiled and Dewy's heart was no longer his: It hadn't been for quite some time.

"Tonight. We sleep in our house tonight!" Ellisa laughed at Dewy's proclamation, and the laughter and joy coming from his parents was not unnoticed.

~~~~~

Late July 1866

Home of Gaius and Tilly Montgomery

Ellisa exhaled loudly. The babe was growing so large she almost couldn't walk. Her ankles were swollen to the point that her shoes no longer fit and her sisters-in-law had leant several dresses that would accommodate her bulging midsection.

"Are you alright, Ellisa?" Emma, Dewy's sister, asked as she rocked her new baby boy in her arms. "You look like you could collapse."

"I tell you what, Emma, I feel like there's four of them in here, and they're all fighting to get out." She laughed, but not much. "It hurts to do anything. I don't know how I manage to roll out of bed, much less take care of the house in this condition. Poor Dewy. He puts up with so much from me."

"They all do. It's no easy task, bringing these babes into the world, Ellisa. You'll be alright."

Ellisa felt a sharp pain start in her back and work its way to the front. "I wish these pains would stop. I think my body is mad at me."

Alarm crossed Dewy's twin's face briefly. "How long has that been happening? I mean, there's pain that goes away, and then there are the pains that don't go away until you have birthed the babe."

"About three days. I can hardly sleep, and Dewy rubs my back and feet every single night. This is misery, for certain."

"Does it take your breath away? I mean, when you get that pain?"

"Yes, Emma." She stopped short as another pain shot through her whole body. Ellisa took a deep breath before sitting down on the settee in the great room. "I wish they'd quit."

"I don't think they're going to, Ellisa. I think you are in the early part of birth. Here, take Mark and I'll fetch Tilly. Don't worry. Everything will be fine."

Ellisa prayed it would be fine. Right now she felt like her body was attempting to rip apart. Mary rushed in, followed by Philip's Emma and Tilly.

"How funny that your babe would choose a Sunday afternoon, when we're all here, to make his debut. Come, we'll get you to the guest room. That's where all the Montgomery's have been born."

Ellisa laughed at Tilly's announcement. "See, you were right. I am going to have a Montgomery in the same place Dewy was born. God has a great sense of humor. OOOH!"

"How often are those pains coming, Ellisa?" Mary asked. She'd done midwifery for many a woman in town since she was out of school.

"It seems to be increasingly close. They were only happening every ten minutes or so. This is the third one in ten minutes."

Mary seemed to take over. "Emma, go tell Dewy and the others that Ellisa's time has come. They'll need to look after the children so we can take care of her. Ma, help me get Ellisa out of her clothing and into a nightshift. We don't want to ruin her..."

"My tent? I could care less if it gets ruined. If this is childbirth, I may not do this again."

All of the others laughed. "We all say that. Wait until your babe is in your arms. You'll have forgotten all the pain." Tilly encouraged.

"Mary," Ellisa gasped, "it's too soon. The babe isn't supposed to come for about five more weeks." Mary patted her hand as she helped her into bed.

Dewy was at the door as they were helping her into the bed. He rushed to her side. "Do you want to go back home?" He asked, obviously unaware of what childbirth entailed.

"There's no time for that, Dewy. Her pains are coming fast and hard. Now go. We'll come get you if you're needed. Go handle the men's work and leave this to us." Mary laughed as she shooed him from the room.

"I don't want Dewy to leave. He put me here, he needs to be here." All of the women laughed again as Mary shut the door.

"We'll bring him in for the birth, okay? Men are funny creatures. They can't handle all of this." Tilly patted Ellisa's hand as Mary checked the progress of the birth.

"It won't be too long. I think your body has been preparing for days."

"Good. I don't want it ... OOOH!" Ellisa's words were cut off by yet another contraction.

~~~~~

3 hours later

Outside, Dewy was beside himself with worry. All of the other men, except Philip, had children, and tried to keep him distracted from the disquiet he felt. Caring for the children seemed to help some, but Dewy still wondered how Ellisa was faring.

Mary came outside, a look of distress marring her features. "Philip. I need you and Jacob to ride for Doc Johnson." The two men nodded, and ran off to saddle the horses.

"Why? What's going on? Lemme see Ellisa. Please?" Dewy said, a little too loudly. His father's gentle, yet firm, grip held his shoulder.

"Don't worry, Dewy. Everything's fine. The baby is breech, and I need Doc to help me turn it. It happens all the time. I just want him to be on hand. Okay?"

"Okay. Can I see her?" The stress in Dewy's voice was evident, causing Mary to take pity on him.

"Go ahead, but be cautioned..." her words were spoken to the wind as he ran off. Mary turned to Gaius. "He's going to lose his stomach."

"Maybe. Maybe he won't. He's been through war. He's seen many atrocities." Gaius, smiling, hugged his daughter.

"Yes, but, not in regards to her. Paw..." Mary was more concerned than she'd let on in front of Dewy. "There's more going on, but I didn't want to worry Dewy unnecessarily. I'll know more when Doc gets here, but he needs to hurry." The two men going for the doctor came out and mounted up at that very same moment. Mary turned to them. "Go quickly. I don't know how much longer she can wait."

Emma, Philip's wife, came out as he rode off. She had only told him just the day before that they were expecting a babe of their own. Her face was pallid, and she seemed more concerned than when Mary had left the room.

"Mary, you're needed." Gaius hugged her with silent encouragement before she ran back to Ellisa's bedside.

Before they went into the room, Mary stopped Emma. "What is it?"

"The water broke." Emma said breathlessly.

"Was it clear in color?" Mary asked.

"Yes, but there's also much more blood than before. And, it seemed like there was more water, almost like it happened twice." She was out of breath, and fear etched her pretty face.

"It will be alright. That's why Doc is coming. I think she's having more than one babe. I hope they won't be too long." Mary said.

~~~~~

Dewy opened the door quietly, saw his mother's face, and almost lost control of his emotions. "How is she, Ma?"

"She's fine, considering she's having a babe." Tilly whispered as she put a cool cloth to Ellisa's forehead.

"Can I have a few minutes with her? Mary sent for Doc. She won't tell me what's wrong. I'm scared, Ma. I spent three years praying she'd take me back, and now that I have her, I don't want to lose her." Dewy's voice cracked on the last two words. Tilly left Ellisa's side and surrounded her baby boy in her arms.

"I'm sure all will be well. She is with Mary and Mary is very good at helping the babe's into the world. And the rest of us are here to help, and to pray. I know it's hard on you men when you can't be in here, but she'll be just fine and in a few more hours, you'll have your child in your arms. The Good Lord knows what he's doing, alright?" Tilly smiled, grabbed Emma's hand and they joined her daughter, Mary, and daughter-in-law, Emma, in the parlor to allow Dewy a few moments alone with his wife.

"Elle?" Dewy whispered, not wanting to awaken her if she was resting. "Elle?" He kissed her forehead.

"Dewy? What are you doing in here? Mary sent for Doc. Did she tell you why?" Ellisa asked breathlessly, trying not to cry out with contractions. She didn't want him to worry. She said as much. "Don't worry. Women have been doing this for thousands of years."

"Why did Mary send for Doc?" He asked in a whisper.

"She thinks I'm having more than one babe. Dewy, we might have twins. Can you imagine?"

His face went ashen, and he felt his knees give just way a little. Then, his face held a smile so bright, it rivaled the sun. "Elle, that is wonderful. I love you, one baby or two. I'm so proud of you! You're so strong."

She gasped and then cried out so loudly that Mary and the other ladies came running in, asking, "What happened?"

"I don't know. She was talking and then that happened." Dewy said as the fear clouded his eyes and gripped his heart.

"It's okay. They should be back with Doc soon. Dewy, you need to go so I can check her progress and try to figure out what happened." Dewy didn't budge from the place where he was sitting.

"Mary, I'm not one to question propriety, and normally I would, but this is Elle, and ..." He just couldn't voice the fears that gripped his mind and heart. If he lost her after all they had been through, he didn't think he'd live.

"I understand, Dewy. I've done this for years, including my own children's birth. Trust God, trust Doc, and trust me. We'll come get you if for a second we think a serious problem arises." Mary nodded and Dewy looked into his sister's eyes; seeing the calm there helped him decide to do as she asked in the midst of Ellisa crying out yet again.

He squeezed her hand, kissed her forehead, and spoke his unending love to his laboring bride before reluctantly leaving the room. His heart stayed behind.

Tilly followed him out, concern for her own child passing that of her daughter-in-law for a moment. "Dewy, if you promise not to make a hole in my floor pacing, you can stay inside to be nearby. But, honestly, you'll be in better company if you're out there with your Paw, Jacob, William, and Philip; that way you can keep busy and maybe even take your mind of what's going on inside. I love you and I promise if there's one problem, we'll send for you, okay?"

"Okay, Ma, and thank you! I'm so scared. She looked like a person moments from death. I still have plenty of those fresh in my mind. All the blood and water, and ..."

"Dewy, trust the Lord. He'll bring her through just like he did me, your sisters, and every other woman who's had children."

"I do trust him, Ma, but I've heard of women dying, too. And babes. I lived through the death of my best friend, but just barely. I couldn't survive losing Elle. My mind would be lost. Promise me you ladies will do everything you can."

"I already have and you know I'm a woman of my word." Tilly hugged her son close before going back inside the guest-turned-birthing room. She prayed Gaius would see the an-guish and anxiety so obvious to her and help their son through this part. Men had no idea what women went through. In her opinion, the husband should be with his wife during the second half of the process. Too often, they were overly anxious to get back to the marriage bed after a woman had given birth. Maybe if they witnessed the birth of their children, they'd wait a little longer and allow her to heal. She giggled at her thoughts.

~~~~~

Dewy went out front and spotted three horses coming up the road; a cloud of dust was the evidence that they'd been riding hard and fast to speed that journey along. He allowed the riders to dismount and Philip took the horse without saying anything as Dewy nodded, shook the Doc's hand and showed him in without uttering one syllable.

Dewy almost made it back into the room when Doc turned, shook his head, and shut the door. Dewy went back outside to greet his Paw and the other men.

~~~~~

Mary greeted Doc. "I think she's having twin babes. One seems to be breech. I felt a foot when I went to check. Much to my chagrin, I pushed it back, but she's in so much pain. Doc, I can't do the delivery I think she needs. You may have to do a Cesarean section. I fear for all three of their lives." She made sure to say so under her breath so Ellisa wouldn't panic.

"Let's see if we can get the babe to turn." Doc smiled and went over to Ellisa's bed side.

"Doc..." Ellisa spoke up. "If you can help it, I want to deliver however many babes God has blessed me with naturally. And, I want

Dewy in here if you have to open me up. He needs to be here. I don't want him to miss this."

Doc nodded first to Ellisa, then to Mary, and lastly to Tilly, who quietly exited the room. He then placed his hands on her belly to gauge position and number. "I feel four bumps. Two are head and two are backsides. So, you are probably having twins, which would explain why you are so large and why you are delivering before your time. Usually, they arrive a little early. No need to fear. You are far enough along that they will survive. Now, Ellisa, take a really deep breath, and let it out very slowly. Mrs. Montgomery," he turned to Emma, Philip's wife, "I want you to count to ten. Ellisa, make the breath last the whole count, understand?" She nodded slightly and inhaled very deeply.

Ellisa tried with all her might as she breathed in to not scream as he moved the babe around in her stomach. Mary was working from the inside, which was even more painful. "Ellisa, I'm going to give you something to help with the pain, and you will be asleep for a little while."

"No, Doc. I don't want that. I'll be alright." She panted. Doc only nodded and continued trying to turn the baby. Tilly came in with Dewy, who rushed to Ellisa's bedside, kissing her cheek and taking her hand in his.

"I think the babe is now in correct position. Next time you feel a pain, take a deep breath, push as hard as you can, and Emma and Dewy will count down from ten to one. Understand, Ellisa?" She nodded, took in a breath as big as her lungs allowed, and began to bare down with everything in her.

After four tries, Doc made her stop, did something that neither Dewy nor Ellisa could see, and said, "One more for me, Ellisa." She did everything again, and paused, and they all waited with bated breath until the first wail came out loud and clear.

"It's a girl!" Dewy dried his eyes and kissed Ellisa.

"Take a break for a moment, Ellisa, and begin again when you're ready."

Mary cleaned the baby up and brought her to Dewy. "She's beautiful. Elle, she looks just like you. Except she's red all over. She has your hair."

Ellisa smiled when Dewy bent low so she could see the baby. "Abigail. It means "father's joy.""

"That's the perfect name. Abigail. Hi, little Abigail." Dewy tears spilled onto his baby daughter's forehead. Ellisa took another sharp breath. "I think the other babe is ready to come now."

"Go ahead and take a deep breath. Someone take the babe so Dewy can help Ellisa." Tilly came over, smiling and crying.

Ellisa inhaled and the others started counting down. Only three pushes and another sweet cry filled the room. "You did it, love. Two babes."

Doc did something before handing the baby to Mary, who did the same with this one as she did with Abigail. "It's a boy!"

"I want to name him after Clem. Clement Jenkins Montgomery." Dewy said before anyone could say differently.

"Oh, Dewy." Emma sobbed out both joy and sorrow as they named their baby after her brother. Dewy took the baby boy and approached Emma. She reluctantly took the newborn.

Doc, who'd begun the process of cleaning Ellisa, had tried to deliver the afterbirth. "Whoa, hold on Ellisa. Don't push just yet." He had a strange, funny look on his face.

Dewy's joyous look turned into one of alarm and dread. "What is it, Doc?" Doc Johnson didn't answer, but put one hand up as if to tell Dewy to wait a moment.

"Ellisa, take another deep breath and push out for me, okay?" She did as the doctor requested. A

"Dewy? What has happened?" Ellisa asked, out of breath and exhausted from the difficult day.

"I- I don't ..." He had no idea what was happening, but his mother was in tears. "Ma?"

"It's a third babe, Dewy. A girl! Triplets!" She gasped. Dewy turned to Ellisa. "She's not breathing." Dewy and Ellisa watched Doc Johnson to see if he would say or do anything. He had a small bundle in a blanket, rubbing the baby's back vigorously. Tilly ran out, but no one knew where.

A minute later, Gaius came in, took the child from the doctor and held her close to his chest. A few seconds later, a slight whimper escaped from the tiny babe, causing all in the room to breathe a sigh of relief. He handed the girl to Ellisa.

"You're blessed. She almost didn't make it. Keep a watch on her for a few days. If you have any problems, send for me directly. Day or night. And, she's going to need help and lots of it for a few weeks, until they figure out how to do this with three wee ones in the home." Doc said after Ellisa had been properly cared for and cleaned.

"Thank you, Doc, Emma, Mary, Emma, and Ma. And you, Paw. How did you know what to do?" Dewy asked quietly, snuggling Abigail and Clement to him at once.

"Your Ma had twins once. The boy, he didn't want to breathe." Gaius laughed. "So, I put you to my chest, Andrew, and stroked your back. You squawked for a long time after that." Laughter went around the room at the image Gaius created. "So, I figured this one was like her Paw and needed a little extra tender loving care. What are you going to name this little blessing?"

"Blessing." Dewy said, as if in a trance. Then, as if someone had slapped him, he jerked his head up. "Let's name her Blessing. For the Good Lord certainly has given her to us."

Ellisa nodded through tears. "Blessing it is. We'll come up with middle names for the girls later. I'm suddenly hungry, thirsty, and sleepy all at once." Dewy bent down and kissed her with such an intimate expression that everyone else in the room averted their eyes.

"I love you, Ellisa. And we have an instant family: Abigail, Blessing, and Clement Montgomery. We should wait a while before we have more children."

"A long while, Andrew Dwight Montgomery. A very long while!" She laughed and closed her eyes.

God had been so good to them. He brought Dewy home; they'd married, built a home, and now had a family. This journey had been long for everyone, and now they were headed in a whole new direction.

~~~~~

Dewy and Ellisa would go on to have seven more children over the space of fifteen years, though no more multiples. They were married over fifty years, living to see the turn of the century and a new era in history. They made it through hard times and enjoyed good times with their loved ones surrounding them. Dewy and Philip became best friends and business partners in industry. Dewy maintained his farm and passed it to his son Clem when he married. Their children all survived to adulthood, and their family had over one hundred people when they passed from life to eternity. Ellisa outlived Dewy by four months, and both went peacefully.

At his life-journey's end, Dewy wrote a book detailing all they'd been through, calling it: "A Prodigal's Return: Love Defined." He dedicated it to four people: His mother; his father - who had welcomed him with love and forgiveness; his brother - who learned what redemption really meant; and of course, his forever bride and the love of his life: Ellisa.

Lightning Source UK Ltd.
Milton Keynes UK
UKHW010639020123
414708UK00014B/719